ZORSAM AND THE GOD WHO DEVOURS

Nick Hayden
Nathan Joseph Sitton Marchand
Aaron Michael Brosman

Cover Art: Jim Faustino of Lungga Creatives

This novella is dedicated to the great people and places of the aptly named city of Story, Indiana, where this tale was first conceived.

Table of Contents

ZORSAM AND THE GOD WHO DEVOURS

CHAPTER 1: The Land of the White Death

Dawn was coming to Skizlag, the land of the white death. The pale tubers withdrew into their holes and crevices as the first gray rays of the sun touched the barren landscape. Bleached bones lay discarded across rock slabs that thrust out from the ground at odd angles. A fresh carcass, large patches of torn skin and tissue covered in blood, marred Skizlag with its color. It had been a thunder lizard, one of those great reptiles from the southern plains whose steps shake the ground and move the earth. Until last night it feared none but the most savage of its brothers.

As the sun struggled over the horizon, red flames of light smoldered on the dry bones and jagged ground. The thunder lizard glistened wet crimson. It shuddered. A tear formed across its protruded belly, which had been left nearly untouched by the tubers in their indiscriminate feast. Wet, bloody hair emerged – a man, shining in fluids, crawled forth from the opening and crouched, tense, expectant. His long hair hung around him. His powerful legs, like a lion's, waited to pounce. His large hands flexed, ready to grab and choke and tear. His black eyes scanned the dead land. Above, carrion eaters circled – not for the thunder lizard, for even carrion eaters did not share meat with the tubers. They circled for him.

Seeing that nothing moved on the ground, the man rose and turned to the thunder lizard. His face, flat, darkened, broad-featured, looked long at the creature that had been his companion and steed in this dread land. He grabbed the large, half-eaten head in his hands, raised his eyes to the sky, and bellowed at the leaden sheet above. Then, after pressing his face against the skull in respect, he continued his journey.

1

He clambered swiftly over the slag, bones, and broken rocks, watching his step, scanning the sky. The carrion eaters followed.

The sun had risen above the rim of the world. Its crimson fire died out, became like the smoke of an extinguished flame. It rose like a blind eye and hung in the sky. The frail twilight lit Skizlag in dimness and blurred the sharp lines of the land.

The man traveled hour by hour, driven by the vision that had visited him, stopping neither for food nor drink nor rest. The cracked, parched land was splintered into a disarray of sharp edges, like a sheet of ice shattered upon the ground. He climbed the protrusions and descended with reckless grace, dropping to a crouch and springing up again without a moment of rest.

The further he went, heaving himself up, sprinting forward, leaping from one foothold to another, the more the space between the upheaved land fell away into dark crevices. He launched himself over the larger chasms, catching himself on the far side and muscling his body onto the next ledge. As the riven landscape grew more fractured, hills of discarded boulders rose to block him. He picked his way up, moving from handhold to handhold, leaping down the other side with the deft movements of a mountain goat. The air lay thick and still about him; the sun, though dim, baked the land. He glistened with sweat.

He stopped. On top of one of these crumbled mountains he stood erect and placed his hand above his eyes. Beyond the sun-bleached land he caught the pale shadow of something immense, an echo of what he pursued. He gazed long to ensure the sight was not an illusion. Satisfied, he continued forward at the same relentless pace.

The hills gave way to a maze of passages sunk into the stone as if a giant hand had drawn lines in the rock with its finger. Some of these ravines ran so shallow that a man could stand in them and rest his arms on the upper ledge. Others sank until the sky remained only a white worm overhead. Passages crisscrossed, rose, sank, and turned at sudden angles. Here the man pressed forward toward the sight he had seen.

When a ravine veered, he continued forward, scaling walls and climbing down again when necessary. Fine, translucent hair covered some of the walls. It swayed hypnotically in the still air, pulsing as with a heartbeat. He used it to ascend and descend. His hands and skin burned afterward.

The light began to grow faint. From the top of one of the crevices he saw the sun sinking toward the far horizon, from whence he had come. He remembered

2

for a moment the trees he had left behind, the cave in the mountains where he slept, his days of killing, eating, sleeping. He glanced upward. The carrion eaters were gone.

For a time, he made progress above the deep trenches, jumping narrow chasms. With bleeding hands, sliced minutely again and again by the fine hair of the chasms, he lowered himself into one too wide for crossing. At the bottom he stopped, listening. A rustle grew in the heavy stillness. In the cracks and splinters of the wall, he could hear the wriggling of tubers. He hurried up the rough rock face. The sound followed as he ran along the surface, as if the creatures tunneled through the stone beneath him. He ran along a shallow trench, the murmur becoming a babble. Twilight deepened. The sun touched the horizon.

A new sound joined the hungry muttering beneath his feet. Stopping, he scanned the sky. The buzz echoed in the shattered land, pierced his ears, rose to a roar – a great insistent screech. He ducked. A giant insect swept over his head and hung a moment motionless in the air. Its body gleamed with a phantom's translucence. The wings beat like a river's rapids. Its stinger throbbed with pleasure. Its many eyes swiveled to study him.

The man seized a rock. As the insect dove, he hurled it. The insect dodged fluidly, so low and quick that though the man spread face first on the ground, the stinger carved a gash into his back. Rolling, he grasped another stone and hurled it at the insect as it turned. This tore a gash in one wing. Flailing in the air, the translucent body darkened to opaque, and livid lines throbbed in jagged paths to converge at the stinger.

The man took a gulp of air just in time. Milky fumes covered him. He closed his eyes as they began to burn. He scrambled along the ground. The rumble of wings followed. It knew where he was and waited for him to succumb to the poison.

His hands found the rim of a trench. Quickly, he began to descend into the gloom below, where no light reached. The cloud of gas blocked the remains of the day; but it did not descend into the darkness. He took a deep breath.

He sensed it the instant before it struck. The tuber shot from the wall like a viper, its senseless maw chomping down where the warrior's hand had been. He clung to the wall with his other. The cliff seemed to writhe as the tubers emerged like monstrous maggots from their many holes. Their pale, sunless bodies showed themselves in the all-but-pitch-darkness. Night had come.

The warrior changed hand and footholds rapidly to escape the voracious jaws. His injured hands left blood on the stone face. The tubers greedily sucked it clean. Below, the floor seethed and slithered, twisted and turned.

But the insect, its angry buzz hovering above, had not forgotten its prey. It dove into the pit, breaking suddenly through its inky discharge, its stinger aimed for him. Roaring, the warrior pushed off from the wall and grabbed hold of the insect's lowest legs, his one hand gripping firmly between the sharp spines. The insect plummeted beneath his weight, and the man raised his legs as he fell toward the thrashing floor. Tubers lifted their bodies, poised by immense muscles, and swayed in anticipation. The warrior kicked them away once, twice, three times, his body hovering six feet from the bottom.

The insect recovered and began to climb. As it flew upward, the man grasped a higher joint of the leg and pulled himself up. The insect flew side to side to shake him off, but the walls of the ravine limited its maneuvers. Dozens of tubers propelled themselves from the walls to catch hold of him. He dodged as he was able, and they rolled off the insect's body. But one sank its teeth into the flying creature's abdomen and did not release.

With this, the insect shot into the air, carrying man and tuber out of the ravine, into the night sky. None of the stars shone. The moon was an eyeless socket. The flying creature careened, and the man hung tight with gritted teeth and taut muscles. He would not let go, not until he landed safely, or the insect fell from the sky, dead. He did not think; like any beast, he acted and reacted; and he never doubted or wavered.

Looking down at the darkened land below, he saw that the labyrinthine plains had given way to a desert of white sand, and from the desert rose the ivory walls he pursued. Hundreds of feet in the air, the man approached his destination by the wild veering of an insect in pain. But the tuber now pierced into the flesh beneath the exoskeleton. The giant winged beast turned aside, lurched, fell, rose unsteadily.

Holding to his precarious grip by one hand, the man stretched out the other and grabbed the base of the insect's stinger. Tightening his huge arms, he drew them together, forcing the leg and stinger to give way beneath the pressure of his strength. The leg moved first, giving the man better leverage with the stinger. He drew his arms together again, slowly. He roared, his body throbbing with vigor and incredible vitality. The stinger snapped off at the base. The warrior, wielding it as a weapon, thrust it deep into the insect, pulled it out, and

4

thrust again. The winged beast descended rapidly beneath the blows, wings fluttering. The white sand rushed up. The man released his grip at the last moment, rolled, and lay still in the sand.

He jumped to his feet, crouched warily. The insect's body lay twitching nearby. The tuber sucked at its exposed innards. Picking up the stinger from where it had landed, the man thrust it through the tuber, pinning it to the insect's body. Two vile creatures would perish together.

He stooped, grabbed a handful of sand, and rubbed it between his fingers. It brought to mind the fire that had raged through the forest. The dead bodies of trees felt like this, gray and thin and dry.

He took stock of his location. He saw the white walls in the distance and started toward them. Nothing moved. With long strides he crossed the desert where nothing lived. He would not stop until he reached those walls… the walls that he had seen in his dreams, the walls that led into darkness.

CHAPTER 2: The Dream-Vision

The man did not have a name. He strode naked across the desert of ash, for he knew not shame. When he asserted himself before a beast, he bellowed and beat his chest. He had no need to declare himself when alone; he simply existed. He knew no language, spoke no words. With grunts, coos, screams, and roars he released his emotions. Even in his mind no vestige of language existed. He thought only images, sharp and gleaming.

The walls he pursued shone prominently in his mind. Three times the image had appeared to him as he slept; three times he had woken in fear, unable to forget the dream. He knew a powerful being had summoned him. This he understood instinctively. On the night of the third dream he began his journey.

He did not linger over memories of his past life, but some images burned brightly within him and rose at mere association. His cave – cold, close, safe; battle – hot, bloody, pitiless; the river's lullaby, the sun's keen gaze; the seductive fingers of darkness, its mystic murmurs; and the angle of branches, the hide of wood, the prick of thorn, the dew of fruit. When he remembered a thing, he tasted it, felt it, heard it as an echo. Sensation was image; image was meaning. Such was his life, a kaleidoscopic succession of experiences, fully felt and little considered. The present dominated his existence.

Indeed, once he began his trek, he considered the dream no more, nor wondered at the meaning of it. He stalked it as prey. Now, he was nearly upon it.

As the night wore on and the white walls drew ever closer, the man quickened his long stride. No creature rose out of the earth to pursue him. The air was clear. By the time he began to run, he believed the area dead to all life. The pale moon rose. It drew again to Earth.

The man approached the white walls. They stretched far, pillars of bone pressed together so tightly that no cracks showed. He ran his hand along them. They were like the femurs of giants: hard, cold, unbreakable, impenetrable. He examined the wall, determined it could not be scaled. Running again, he followed the wall for a long time, finding no entrance or handhold. Eventually he came to the corner of the wall, saw no change, and continued to follow its lines.

The moon set. No sun appeared. A profound darkness settled over the land and even the man's sharp eyes struggled to determine shapes in the blackness. The wall remained a steady boundary of gray.

He turned another corner. Partway along this side, a black opening interrupted the pallid expanse of bone. It gaped at him. Cold air blew from within. He entered. It seemed as if he moved against a current. He stopped and looked back. He saw no more behind than ahead.

Raising his arms, he roared and announced himself to the one who had summoned him. He waited and roared again. After the third challenge, he paced boldly forward, his arms at his side, confident in his direction even in the dark. He had explored deeply into the cave that had been his home and had gained a sixth sense of unlighted spaces.

As he walked, he could feel the walls drawing nearer, funneling him into a single path. The air itself seemed to constrict around him. The darkness weighed upon him, like deep water. Soon, he could touch cold stone on either side. Imperceptibly, the walls pressed in until they scraped his shoulders. He turned sideways when the way became too narrow. For a long time, he squeezed between the rough faces, cutting his chest and arms beneath the sharp fingers of uneven rock, never considering that he might turn back.

With a final push, he found himself wedged in place. Flexing his massive muscles, twisting and turning, he tried to dislodge himself. He could not. He roared, the air passing through his iron lungs. The whole cavern seemed to shake. Again and again he cried out, demanding satisfaction. His body oozed blood from his many cuts; his limbs ached from the brutal bruises he inflicted by his movements. These only fueled his expectation of an answer.

When the answer came, he fell silent. The sound of it was unlike any he had heard before. Stranger still, it communicated beneath the raw, visceral passions that formed the dance between him and the beasts of the world. It was as if vision suddenly returned to him in the depths of darkness.

The sound that reached his ears was a voice like a cold wind – "You can go no further as you are." And he understood.

He stood there, unable to respond, not knowing *how* to respond. The voice had been neither challenge nor comfort. In humility, the man imitated the song of water passing lazily over stone.

"You cannot speak." The voice seemed to surround him, pressing more tightly than the stone. "It does not matter. Every creature, alive or dead, understands me. Why are you here? Envision it. I will see it if you allow me."

When the man heard the words *"you cannot speak,"* he did not understand what the voice meant, but the image in his head gleamed brightly for a moment. It pained him as if he looked into the sun. He did not want to look away. But when the voice said, *"envision it,"* he understood. He vividly recalled the dream that had summoned him, the white walls, towering over the desert, everything still and empty and dead. It was only an image, but in his dreams he had approached it futilely for hours in growing frustration and dread.

"How have you come here?"

And, scene by scene, he recalled his journey, the long days beneath the jungle canopy; the cool streams in the rising hills; rocks and snow and wind as he climbed; rocks and snow and wind as he descended; wide plains of grass covered with beasts; thunder lizards who scattered the herds and caused the earth to quake; pain, rage, exhaustion as he fought the indomitable beast; domination and submission; weeks upon the lizard's back, wind in his face, the sea of grass beneath; the first fingers of Skizlag corrupting the plains; darkness, tubers, terror, blood; a night in the belly of the beast for shelter; slag, crags; the wasps, the flight, the white walls – *now*.

As the last image faded, the voice rose from the darkness. "None before have come here by that path. I did not believe that any could. Now you have gone as far as is possible in your state. From here, the path becomes still narrower, descends still deeper, until not even the smallest of creatures might pass. But plenty do pass. I have come from there and to that place I will return.

"It is evident you have been sent, but it is to me you have been sent and not to that place. You cannot enter there. But there is another place it has been given me to watch over where the living sometimes come to rest. I will lead you there if you are certain you wish to follow the vision. But I must warn you, you may learn much you do not know and lose some of what you now possess. If you come with me, you will never again have the strength to do what you did in coming here. This is my warning. Do you come?"

The man assented in his way. The voice touched him upon the forehead with a word cold and deep, deeper even than image, and he fell asleep.

CHAPTER 3: The Three Lessons

When he woke, he found himself in a chamber of gloom and fog. A strange light emanated darkly from the thick clouds, like firelight reflected off billows of black smoke. The fog clung to his skin – as he stood, it seemed to rise with him. When he walked, streamers stubbornly trailed behind, but slowly, like tatters of cloud blown by high, distant winds.

He did not seem to be in a room, but in a space; not in a cavern, but in an expanse of sky. He could not see the ground on which he stood, and when he bent to examine it with his hands, he found nothing. He could grasp the heels of his feet, but not the surface upon which they rested.

The man cried out, seeking the power that had summoned him here. It had called by dream and vision. He had come, recognizing its authority. He believed in sorcery – one could not live in untamed lands without sensing the deep breathings of powers beyond sight. He had no image for these intrusions except a memory of screaming at a storm in earlier years, an old memory he avoided. He cried out again, angrier this time. The mists rose up before him, condensed into the form of a man. He stepped back. He had never before seen another like himself.

No – quickly, he recognized his mistake. The being before him stood on two feet like a man, and in proportions he resembled a man, but his hands were bone and his face a skull. Black cloth covered his body in tatters and a circlet of gold rested upon his head. Two wings hung from the folds of his arms, like those of a bat.

The mouth did not move when he spoke. "You are not afraid?"

A guttural shout of defiance and pride answered.

"We have met before. Do you remember?"

The man wanted only one thing, to find the one who had summoned him. Power must be respected or overthrown. The man shouted his challenge and danced before the skeleton as a male dances to show his strength. Powerfully, savagely, he roared as he circled the strange being. Wildly, he turned and raised his hands and grunted a primal rhythm.

The dark figure interrupted. "It is not for me that you dance. You act out of ignorance. You must remember all you have forgotten. Be still."

The man stopped because the other had spoken with authority. He turned his head away in submission. The cold claw of the other grabbed his face. And he remembered:

***

Men dance around a large fire and sing to the Great One. Outside this circle, others stand. They are like the men but different – shorter, smaller, softer. A child holds the hand of one of these. The child is he, and he holds his mother's hand as she sings. He speaks to her. The words are crude, simplistic, both sounds with meaning and sounds without mixed together, each tinged with awe and excitement. It is not unlike how he now communicates.

He, too, tries to dance, bobbing his little body and twisting unsteadily in a circle. The fire illuminates the dancers and illuminates him. His mother smiles, and he tugs her hand to make her dance, too. She does a little, one hand in his, the other on her belly, swollen with child...

***

The vision faded away. The man stood transfixed. The skeletal face of his guardian watched him silently, but the man relived the vision. Then his black guardian spoke, as if he too saw the vision, and the guardian detailed what he saw, repeating the words again and again. The words melded with the image and shone upon the figures in his mind. *Mother. Child. Family. Worship. God.*

"Father?" He had seen the man near the fire, had seen that special look and heard the word from the fleshless lips. And, for a moment, the safety he knew in the word seemed equal to the power of this strange being.

11

"No," answered the skull. "I am not he. But you are not the first to think of me in this way. You do so because you do not understand. Most do so out of fear. You have seen enough for now. You must absorb what you have learned. Rest. I will return in time."

The figure glided away, fading into the fog. The man, suddenly weary with the weight of his new knowledge, sat among the dark clouds and closed his eyes. The vision returned. He could explore it, observe everything, hear again the names the guardian had given each object.

He slept. Time seemed to pass, but whether little or much, or none at all, he did not know. When he woke, he was standing. The skull met his eyes. The cold, bony hands gripped his own.

"Do you know what you saw?"

"Yes." He spoke. For a fleeting moment, it seemed strange to him, like waking in an unusual place.

"There is more." The hand reached up, clutched his head tightly. He saw.

***

Dancing. The same night as before... or, a different one? A loud call, not a beast, but a tone – a trumpet. Horse hooves, ferocious cries, shouts. The music ends. The dancing ceases. For a moment, everyone is still. He cannot understand what is happening. The trumpet cries again, closer, almost in his head. Everyone begins to move as riders enter the circle. His mother lifts him, flees with him. He can see the battle over her shoulder. Weapons – axes, swords, clubs, staves – flash and crack in the hands of the men.

A black horse rears, its rider raises his sword in triumph. A frightful helmet covers his face – a skull. His father defiant, sword raised, engages in battle with the rider. The rider's sword enters flesh, exits red. His father falls. He is crying, shouting, *Dadda! Dadda!*" But his mother is carrying him away, and the dead cover his father.

***

The image hung vividly in the air. The man's eyes roved frantically over the scene. Blood he understood. Battle he knew. But a great revelation enveloped him, and he could not grasp the immensity of it. He had never before loved as a child loved; he had forgotten it. Neither had he suffered loss as a child does; he had hidden it.

He saw his guardian's white face, and he remembered the rider in black. He raised his arms, placed his hands around the other's neck, and squeezed.

"Enemy!" he roared. The beast's anger intermingled with the human's need for justice.

"You are not the first to call me so. I am no friend of man, but I am no enemy of the Great One," said the other, unhindered by the man's attack. "You cannot harm me. Think on what you have seen. You have seen both love and hate, but there is still more. You must learn everything you are. You cannot fulfill your purpose otherwise. I will return to teach you again."

The guardian waited. After many long minutes, the man released his grip, and the other faded into billows of dark smoke. The man could not keep his eyes open.

He slept fitfully, the wild light and shadows of growing fires distorting the images of battle. They passed through his brain at frightful speeds. He saw everything, every expression of fear and courage, every attack and parry, every drop of blood that spilled to the ground. He saw the terror and sorrow in his own childish eyes. Crimson stained the memories; fire fueled the remembrance.

He woke, panting hard, his nails digging into his calloused palms. Even awake he could not be rid of the violence and destruction. What tormented him were not the images alone; he did not hate battle or gore. But with the images came new words, weighty words that troubled him and did not settle. Before, in his old life, events happened, and he did not consider the reason why or the rightness of the event. He slew a beast because it hunted him. He ate because he hungered. He thirsted and drank. He wanted and acquired. His world was immediate, visceral, physical, tactile, and nothing more. He had sensed great powers in the world; he had sensed powers in himself. These he placated with fear and awe and pressed forward.

But these words transformed his world. Suddenly, life existed beyond him, deeply rooted, with branches far above his understanding. Now pain existed as a theory as well as in the moment of suffering. Eating became a ritual. He knew "I" and "others" – man and beast, want and desire, love and choice. What had been direct and simple became something more.

13

A new dimension deepened every facet of the world: morality. Before, there had been yes and no. Language introduced him to right and wrong, because the words themselves made such distinctions.

He lay a long while, letting the words in his soul find their places. They changed his world, but his directness and simplicity remained. His newfound morality allowed no ambiguity. And he knew now what he must do next.

He stalked through the dark mists, growling out of habit, searching for the black guardian of that place. The skeletal being appeared beside him as he walked.

"I have taught you nearly all I have been assigned to teach. Whatever remains will be taught you by other means and at other times."

"Where are the enemies?" the warrior demanded. "I must punish them. It is just."

The other touched him lightly on the shoulder. "You understand in part. You will soon see why you were sent to me – I, who have never spoken to a human as I now speak to you, as if we were companions. You may still misunderstand, but the one who sent you will explain. Now, are you ready to receive the final lesson?"

"Release me from this place. I must seek out the ones who destroy without reason."

"You will stay a little longer. At the end of the appointed time, you will be free to do as you please. First, I must complete the work assigned me. Are you willing?"

The man said nothing, expecting his guardian to proceed without hesitation. If this is what must be done to leave, he would do it. The guardian did not touch his head.

"Why do you not do it?" the man demanded.

"I asked if you are willing. Before, I taught you as a child who must be forced to learn. Now I teach you as a man who may choose. If you are willing, I will teach. If not, I will not."

"Do it," the man said.

The cold, thin fingers touched his skull. He remembered.

ZORSAM AND THE GOD WHO DEVOURS

***

It is that night again, full of fire and blood. His mother lifts him in her arms as she flees from the battle. He sees nothing distinctly. He is confused, frightened. His mother stops. They are at the well outside the village. She sets him down, shouts at him, tells him not to move as she drags up the bucket.

"Come here," she commands. She seems angry; he is crying. She sees it, scoops him up, kisses him fiercely. "I love you, Zorsam." She squeezes him tight. He can feel the warmth of her body. Then she places him in the bucket. He starts to get out, but she shakes her head and begins to lower the rope. "Stay! Zorsam, stay! No, stop – stay!" Tears shine red in the firelight from the village. He cries, calling out for his mother. "Be quiet, Zorsam! Be quiet! Don't cry. Be quiet!"

The tone of her voice causes him to cry the louder. The bucket settles in the water below, and he floats unsteadily in his little boat. The well's opening is high above, showing nothing but dark sky. He weeps hysterically for a time, calling for his mother, until he can barely catch his breath. He falls silent but continues to weep. Voices echo down to him from above. He waits in terror. The rope tightens. Without thinking, he jumps from it. He hears only terrible laughter.

He is young and has only swum with others, never alone. His mother does not let him swim alone. There is a current to the cold water. It pushes him to the wall, dragging him down. When he stretches his foot, he feels where the stone wall ends. The water continues down beyond his reach. He clings desperately to the uneven rock.

The bucket never returns.

For a long time, he clings to that wall. He begins to shiver within the first hour. Still, he removes his clothes, so they do not drag him down. At the end of three, his hands ache so badly he can think of nothing else. He has no plans, no hopes, only an instinct for survival. The tiny opening above shows only night; day does not come.

He has long since stopped crying. His face is solemn, like a man's. He knows that soon he must let go and sink. Beyond that, he knows nothing. An hour later, the strange calm has passed away. He breathes sharply, shallowly, as if already

15

drowning. He repeats the lyrics the women sing while the men dance, barely understanding the praise to the Great One. His fingers keep slipping.

It begins to rain. He knows because he feels a few drops on his head. This is it – this is the end. He wails, holding nothing back, crying out because he can do nothing else.

Suddenly the water begins to rise. It happens so quickly he feels it as a swell. Whatever underground river feeds the well is rising. It washes over him. Spluttering, he reaches for a new handhold. The water continues to surge upward. He gasps for air. He cannot keep above the waterline. His exhausted limbs struggle to keep him afloat. The mouth of the well gapes wider. The water rises no more.

Above, he can see light behind the rain clouds. The stone wall is chipped and cracked here, torn open by roots and some tremor in years past. With a cry of pain, he lifts himself out of the water by his arms. His feet slip, then find a hold. His tears make it hard to find a place for his hands. He rests, the water below him receding now.

He looks up. The clouds are blowing swiftly past. With a great effort, he ascends a body length, then one more. He grips the lip of the well. He heaves, pulls himself up, flops over, and finds himself on his back, unable to catch his breath. The gray light of day touches the sky.

He falls asleep. The village smolders nearby. He sleeps so soundly he might be taken for one of the dead.

CHAPTER 4: Among the Dead

He woke in darkness. He was no longer a little boy. He was a man, at least twenty. His name was Zorsam. It took him time to collect his thoughts. The nameless warrior who had received the vision of the bone walls had been swallowed by the man Zorsam. With this last lesson he had not only received an identity, he had gained a community. Just as he had realized "I" before, now he understood "we." With a name, he became fully human; as a human, he became one of many. He had discovered his soul, and having found it, he discovered his family as well.

The joyful weight of that knowledge kept him in a state of awe. He had been anchored to something greater than himself. But hatred, too, had begun to grow, worming through the unexplored depths of his conscience. In understanding all he had forgotten, all that raised him above the beasts, he learned the deep darkness of man. As a beast, he attacked those who attacked him; as a man, he planned vengeance on those who injured those he loved. The first was instinct; the second, judgment.

When he finally shook himself from his thoughts, he sat up. The fog and darkening light remained, but a sense of reverence permeated the air. This struck him deeply. In his previous savagery, he had bowed before large trees, the burning sun, powerful felines as they hunted. This air of holiness was truer than what he had before deemed worship, and he was ashamed of his ignorant days. He got to his hands and knees and moaned softly. He sensed the shapes of others nearby, prostrate also. He could not see them. His head was bowed, his eyes averted. The voice of the guardian reached him.

"Your worship is seen and honored. Rise. You do not bow to me, but that is obvious to you. I have come to speak with you one last time."

Humbly, Zorsam stood. His powerful arms and legs pushed him up, and he reveled in the simple action. He felt stronger than he ever had. Taking in the scene at a glance, he saw men and women lying upon their backs as if asleep. A faint light emanated from them.

"You are Death," Zorsam said.

Death nodded. "That is one of my names."

"I met you in the well."

"I was close to you that night, but it was not the time ordained for you."

"Is this your domain?"

"This is one place I have been given authority. Here, men and women come who approach the end of mortal existence. They may yet live if it is the Great One's will. He decrees all things. I am merely a servant. He has chosen you to be a servant also."

"Let me talk to him. I will listen to what he has to say. If it pleases me, I will do as he asks."

"You are not able to talk with him face-to-face. You are capable only of speaking to Death in that way. You cannot speak to the Glory. But I will tell you what he has chosen you for. You are to be the sword in his hand, just as I am, to bring wrath upon those whose evil has reached full measure. We are servants of necessity and last resort, but we are true servants nonetheless. Come, look upon this woman."

The black figure motioned to a young woman nearby. She was clothed in gloom, but her face was visible. Her skin was dark and smooth, her hair black, her lips full. The lines of her neck showed strength; the soft curve of her cheeks hinted at joy. He wondered what light he would find in her eyes. He had found what he had feebly missed in his ignorant state and what he now truly desired – another like himself. He bent over her, touched her face with the curiosity and impudence of a child. She did not wake.

"Who is she? What is her name?"

"Her name is Asundi. She is a daughter of your people. She lies here from injuries inflicted by King Margruxks, ruler of the lands of Glaur. It is he who massacred and enslaved your people – the last people to fall. For more than fifteen years they have bent beneath his rod and whip. They dig deep holes for their inverted palaces, in which he, his priests, and his officials live. They also labor at the great tower that is to reach the heavens." Death lifted his hand. "May I?"

"Yes."

Death raised his finger to Zorsam's forehead. The darkly clad figure's cold touch pierced him. What he saw now was not a memory, as before, but something else, like the half-formed images conjured by a smell or a familiar scene. One after another, sense layered on sense, confused like ravens arguing, came imagery of smoke and blood, charred houses and bodies, screams and lashings and broken bones, unwanted hands, knees forced to bend, heads bodiless on the ground, ropes, chains, blades, mud, tears, nakedness, and night.

Death removed his hand. "Many of the innocent have passed through this realm, and I have seen their suffering. I have seen Asundi's, too. She suffered many blows in her capture, for she and others like her are to be offered to Manrix, the God Who Devours. She is a virgin, a princess among the beaten ranks of your tribe. For years, your people, and the tribes of many lands, have been crying out to the Great One. He has chosen you to be the strength of his right arm."

Zorsam studied the woman intensely. His sudden possessive desire for her grew with Death's words. He hated Margruxks and all who served him. They destroyed wantonly; they captured virgins, violated them, slaughtered them. He roared, his arms of iron raised in defiant decision, his face a gruesome mask of rage. He roared again, louder, lifting his face to the ceiling, to the world above, where he would wreak vengeance.

Death spoke. "You may stay if you like, but I will no longer keep you here."

"I will leave. Show me the way."

"Come." Death took Zorsam by the hand and led him by cunning paths through the darkness. At times they would come among groups of men and women. Death bent over one or two and helped them gently to their feet. They followed in silence. In time, dozens gathered around Death and obediently followed.

"Are you returning to the world?" one asked Zorsam.

"Yes."

None of the others spoke.

Death stopped. He reached into thick clouds, found some surface, and pushed. A door opened outward into darkness.

19

"This is where you enter the world again. Continue upward, and you will find light. I can help you no further. I must lead these souls to another place, where they will await judgment. I do not judge. I treat all equally."

"I thank you for what you have returned to me. I lost all when I was in the well. Now you have restored me."

Death shook his head. "I only take. Whatever you have been given has been given by the Great One. Will you tell me why I showed you the third vision?"

"So that I would know myself. So that I know what I suffered and what I endured. So that I know what I survived and why I avenge."

Death stared deep into Zorsam's eyes. Zorsam did not turn away from the awful depths of those sockets.

"The danger of being taught by Death is that you might become like him. I am enough for all the world. The vision of the well was not given for your sake or for mine, but for His who gives life. The Great One raised you out of that hole. He gave you strength to live. Remember that. Now go."

Zorsam left through the opening and traveled through deep caverns, always ascending, seeing nothing in the darkness, hearing nothing. He did not tire as he climbed; his strength remained inexhaustible. His time in the depths had fully replenished him. He ascended steadily, sometimes pulling himself hand over hand up steep inclines. All the while he could feel the deep earth disappearing below him, feel the weight of the earth falling away, as if he were straining for the surface after diving for some mollusk on the lake floor.

He saw dim light. It grew, brightened, and overwhelmed him. Blinking, shielding his eyes, he pressed forward. The sun stood above him. Red rock and sand burned in the heat. His skin basked in the warmth. He stood naked, his powerful chest heaving, his face full of triumph and wonder. He looked upon the world as if for the first time. The land shone with light and knowledge; with memory, meaning, and challenge. He bellowed, full of joy and a sort of fierce possessiveness. The world was his, and he had strength to do as he wished.

The cave had led Zorsam to a depression in the earth, a bowl of burning red sand and rock. He climbed the slope. Exposed, he became conscious of his nakedness and knew he needed clothing.

At the top of the bowl, he found himself at the bottom of a barren canyon. He stood at one end, three sheer walls of red rock surrounding him. The passage widened to the south, the canyon walls slithering away. The stench of death met him. Crumpled forms lay discarded on the ground. He ran to them and there witnessed his fellow man for the first time beneath the sun. They lay twisted and maimed, dark stains of blood deepening the already crimson ground.

Flies buzzed in dark clouds, driven to the air at his coming, settling back like shrouds at his stillness. There were nearly fifty corpses, their bellies bloated, their eyes rolled in their head. Gashes streaked their bodies in profusion. Zorsam knew with certainty that the savagery had not finished when these men had died.

Death's passage led to fields of death. Zorsam understood this.

He walked among the bodies, looking them over carefully. The vultures had flown away, but the maggots continued their feasting. He thought he saw the twitch of a hand. He stopped and studied the man; his eyes were closed. An animal might still react when dead. No – the chest trembled with the agony of breath. Zorsam knelt beside him.

"Who did this?"

The dying man's lips tried to form words. "Why am... I... alive?"

"Who did this? Was it Margruxks?"

"His work... we refused to do it..." The man could not get air.

Zorsam waited. From time to time, hoarse exhalation left the dying man, half-syllables with incomprehensible meaning. His hand brushed Zorsam in a sudden spasm and came to rest. Zorsam followed the movement of the hand and found a sword nearby. He stood to retrieve it and for the first time felt the weight of iron. He wielded it easily. He understood how it might aid him, like the tail of a scorpion or sudden strike of a serpent.

Returning to the dying man, and understanding him to be one of his people, Zorsam slew him to end his pain. Kneeling again, he grabbed the man's head in his hands, looked to the burning sun, and moaned over the dead.

Standing, he examined the sword. "This weapon will not fail in my hands, my friend."

He stood rooted in place, staring still at the dead. Animals could be left to rot; he believed that man should not. Lodging the sword deep in the sand, he lifted the dead man in his arms and carried him down into the cave. There, Death could honor the bodies. One by one he carried the men to their dark grave.

Among their possessions he found a small loaf of bread, which he ate. He took nothing else from them except a tattered robe, which he ripped and tied around his waist. It was night when he finished. He sang laments among the bodies, songs learned from sorrowful birds, and he danced his old primal dances of mourning and death. He slept in the canyon above.

Before first light, he woke and descended to the cavern mouth. The bodies had been ushered away in the night. Returning to the canyon, he found the trail the murderers had left. It would lead him to Glaur, and to Margruxks. He started forward, somber and growing in hatred.

CHAPTER 5: Into the Killing Fields

With feral speed, Zorsam howled through the canyon, the wind whipping at his face. It carried the stench of death. Bodies littered the path of blood and destruction he followed. He would have no trouble finding his prey.

The men had been butchered as they ran. It was *wrong*. Zorsam had never before used the word; he had never witnessed such unfettered brutality. He felt the presence of Death, ushering the longsuffering to their new home.

I must race the sun. I will hunt this murderer and slay him, and there shall be justice.

Zorsam's feet quickened, his anger flaming. It took no skill to track his prey. Victory had made them reckless. They believed themselves safe.

He wound through cracks and crevices, passages the slain had hoped to use to slow their pursuers. He did not slow, and as he thought of Margruxks' blood upon his sword his rage brought him untold stamina. Sharp stones cut his feet, and red sand stung his eyes. He did not take heed. For hours and countless steps he endured, letting the pain sharpen him. Soon, he could no longer sense Death's presence.

Death cannot keep pace with me. Do not worry, my teacher, I will send others to tell you I am well. Your instruction will not be wasted.

As the cliffs opened, a river crashed down from the heights in clouds of spray. Below, the water was cool and clear. Its banks were churned by feet, the fleeing and the pursuers marking their way. Zorsam quenched his thirst. He followed the stream and the trail of Margruxks' men as they left the canyon. The stream flowed into a great ocean.

Many miles over the water, a dark mass of clouds writhed and sparked. He had seen great thunderheads and storm clouds of relentless power, but never had he seen the ocean nor the sky united with it in such fury. He would need shelter. If he was caught on the beach in such a storm, it would pound him into the rocks or drag him into the sea. He had lost the trail in the soft sand and grass of the beach.

As he continued, it began to rain, the storm sweeping in. It was warm rain, offering no refreshment. Lightning struck the cliffs that hemmed him in. Rocks splintered and crashed into the wet sand. That was where he would climb.

The rain deepened. He flung himself against the cliff face and began his ascent, water streaking down his body, erasing the grime and sweat of his pursuit. With strong fingers he gripped the slick rock and, in time, pulled himself to the top, sheets of rain slashing across his body. It mattered not, no more than a fly buzzing about his head. He stood above the brunt of the storm. Now was the time to find shelter.

Zorsam had feared he had lost the trail before ascending to the heights. He had been wrong.

The field before him was littered with bodies. The mud was still stained with blood that thickened the growing puddles. The men had been cornered against the cliff. He bent close to examine bodies. Many had been kneeling when slain. They had tried to surrender. They had been killed anyway. He could smell the blood in the warm, thick air, and the rotten odor of death. Some had escaped down the cliff, but most had not.

For the first time since emerging from Death's Lair, he hesitated. Animals were slain for food or clothing. These men were slain pitilessly. Perhaps a few still lived who could tell him details of what had happened. He searched among the corpses for some sign of life, wiping away the water streaming down his forehead. Through the haze of the storm he saw the waves pummel the beach and the dark form of bodies tossed upon the sand then pulled back to their watery grave.

Turning back to the field, he saw movement. He crouched down and peered through the torrent. He saw two figures moving carefully in the distances. They were small and bent over and moved from body to body. Zorsam crawled forward on hands and knees until he was close enough to hear their voices over the fury of the storm.

"Heya! Rask! You's gotta come see. Dees guys musta been sumbody. Look at dis sword!"

"Mosda dees ain't got no weapons. Is strange. I tells you, Gleen, is not right, dat's de truth."

"Na, what's not right, Rask, is dat we's stealin' from de dead. We's use ta be proud. Heaven's weepin' for us, dat's the truth."

Gleen raised his hands to the sky then returned to rummaging through a woman's pockets.

"No, Gleen, I's serious dis time. Somedin's not right 'bout dis."

Zorsam gripped his sword. Where the dead were, there came vultures, filthy and weak creatures who could not survive by strength. These two would tell him what he needed to know.

He stood and lightning struck, a pillar of light and fire that blinded him. He shut his eyes against it and stepped back from its heat. When he looked again, a third man stood in heavy armor. The hilt of a massive sword showed over his shoulder.

"It has been decreed that all rats shall be exterminated," the warrior said. "It'll be a pleasure to finally see you dead. How long have you plagued us, Rask? A year? Gleen, how many months have you sought your fortune in a dead man's pockets? The king has grown tired of you."

With a great cry he drew his sword and slashed it in one motion. The two men jumped back with the speed of prey and crouched down. The warrior looked at them, and in the lightning Zorsam saw him smile.

"Why'd de king mess wif us? We's less dan beggas," Rask cried out. "He's got our homes and lands. What's a couple men's lives 'gainst dat?"

"We's not worf it," Gleen said. "We's leavin,' alright?"

"You had your chance. Your prince bent his knee. You refused. Now your prince commands an army. What do you have? Filth, famine, and disease." The warrior lifted his sword again. "And now you shall have death."

Gleen ran.

As Zorsam watched, the warrior's eyes began to shine with the blue of deep night. Sheathing his sword, he raised his arms, stretching them out as if he meant to grasp the storm. Lightning struck him and he caught it, collected it, balled it up between his hands. He lowered his arms, tossing the sparking mass of light from one hand to the other as if testing its weight.

"You will have to scurry faster than that," the warrior intoned.

Gleen had increased his distance, but it made no difference. With a flick of the wrist, the warrior tossed the ball of lightning to the ground, where it rolled after the fleeing man. It bound after him faster and faster, swifter than a gazelle, gaining size until it smashed into him.

Gleen fell dead, convulsing as smoke rose wet and black from his skin.

Rask remained still in the same position, pinned by fear. Zorsam cared nothing for this little man, but the warrior killed wantonly and mocked the dead. Now he would have to deal with Zorsam.

Zorsam jumped and landed between the warrior and Rask.

"Who is this?" the warrior asked with a sneer.

The rain lessened, and for a moment the thunder was silent. The storm waited.

"You set a trap for a rat, but you have caught a lion," Zorsam said. "The Great One will judge you for your cowardice."

"The Great One!" laughed the warrior. "He is dead. Manrix has devoured him. The last of his worshippers have been decimated. Their princesses have been slaughtered to feed Manrix's appetite."

Zorsam ran to close the distance, sword raised above his head. The warrior gathered lightning and let it loose in one motion. The electricity struck Zorsam in the chest and tremored through him. His muscles tensed painfully, and he could smell his burnt flesh. The rain once again drove down in solid sheets.

Zorsam forced his muscles to obey him. He lifted his sword once again and pressed forward, roaring.

The warrior dropped his hands to the ground, letting the lightning slip away, and stomped down with his foot. A shock wave radiated from his position, but Zorsam had expected some trick. He leapt into the air and swung down with all his force. The warrior stepped back to steady himself and just managed to unsheathe his sword in time. A shudder of metal rang through the air. Zorsam snarled, pressing his sword close.

"In Glaur, we beat animals like you till they obey," the warrior mocked, managing to push Zorsam away.

Zorsam lowered his body, ready to charge. "My spirit is iron. You will be crushed upon it."

The warrior lunged at Zorsam before he could pounce, but Zorsam dodged with feline fluidity. With swing and thrust, the warrior attacked Zorsam, but

Zorsam dodged and parried and like a serpent, darted in with his great tooth, cracking armor and finding flesh.

"The Great One is not dead. He sent me. I will send you to him."———

The great warrior pulled back a moment. Lightning struck his sword and wreathed it with pulsing energy. Zorsam rushed in, unafraid. The great sword slashed for his head, but Zorsam rolled to the ground and plunged his sword up through his adversary's body, beneath armor, within ribs, through the heart.

The warrior slumped onto Zorsam's sword and died. It took only a moment to remove the weapon and push the body onto the ground to join those he had slain.

Zorsam stood drenched in rain, covered in mud, his sword bloody, and howled in victory.

When he looked down, Rask huddled at his feet, staring at him.

"You loot the dead. You disgrace the bravery of better men. What right have you to live?"

Rask edged away from Zorsam but stumbled over a body buried in the grass and mud.

"None. I's got none."

"What happened here? Why this slaughter?"

"Is Margruxks. Dis his doin'. He marchin' dat way and had prisoners. Dey too slow. Dat's what he said." He trembled beneath Zorsam's gaze. "You's gonna kill me?"

"I am not the judge of such as you. Your people have been wronged."

"Yea, dey has. But what's kin I do?"

"You may not right wrongs. *I* am the Great One's sword."

"Den maybes I kin helps you out?"

"If the Great One sends you with me, I will not argue."

"Who's dis Great One?"

"He is the one who sent me. He showed me who I am and told me what I shall do." Zorsam swung his sword in a slow arc to indicate the killing field. "Those who did this lived without fear. They will learn fear. That is why I am sent. Who else has stood before the ravenous Kranathi serpent? Who else has tamed the great Northern thunder lizard? The Great One has fashioned me to strike the heart of Margruxks."

"Well, den I like dis Great One. I come wif you. Tonight, you come wif me, tho. I know a cave we kin use."

27

That night was the first Zorsam spent with another person. Rask was not strong enough to hurt him. That allowed him to lower his guard and enter the small space with him. Huddled in the small cavern, Rask fell asleep. Zorsam watched him, this man who lived off others, the prey whom he had saved. He did not know what to think of this man, who did not quite seem a man. The storm continued and finally Zorsam rested, his hand upon the hilt of his sword.

CHAPTER 6: The Chase

The sun rose upon a wet and beaten world. Zorsam and Rask emerged onto the muddy fields in the early morning light. The storm had subsided hours earlier and only stray wisps of cloud still clothed the sky.

Zorsam looked upon Rask clearly for the first time. He was a puny man, so short that he barely came up to Zorsam's chest. Tatters of cloth pieced together by ingenuity enclosed him like the scales of a baggy reptile. He smelled of death, not of a predator's breath, but of swamp and decay.

Something else he noticed – a heaviness to Rask's gait, a darkness upon his words. It was not a physical thing, but it was a real thing, and as Zorsam watched the small man hunt for some scraps of food, he began to understand. It was grief and the shadow of death.

This struck Zorsam, for it seemed to him men should be filled with life until Death touched them upon the shoulder and led them into shadowlands. As Rask scavenged, Zorsam looked to the ocean beyond and knelt to pray to the Great One, the god of his people, for this day and for the life that was in him and for the purpose he had been given. It was a straightforward prayer, not of words but of deep emotion. His roar echoed across the field and ascended into the sky.

"You shouldn' do dat," Rask said, scurrying over at the sound. "De king will come. You've slain his man. He's a comin' fer you fer sure."

"Fear not, small man. I carry the sword of the Great One."

"If you say so. An' where does de Great One want us ta go, eh?"

"After the soldiers."

"What fer?"

"To seek out Asundi."

"And de Great One shows you dis?"

"Death showed me."

"He did, did he? I know where de army is, if you's goin' dat way."

"We go east."

"I knows. Dey's headin' dat way ta make der sacrifices ta Manrix."

"Then talking is done. We go."

Zorsam began to run.

"Blast!" Rask shouted, following after. "I never asked yer name."

"It is Zorsam."

With a panther's stride Zorsam raced into the rising sun. Across the bloodied plains he swept. Rask kept pace with his short legs, gasping, and Zorsam raced effortlessly. Hour by hour he ran, with hardly a break except for a drink of fresh water when he encountered it. He understood that he must move, that he must neither hesitate nor linger, for he felt the ominous pressure of time upon him. He ignored hunger and fatigue, reveling instead in the swift beat of his heart and the burning of his muscles. There was pleasure in exertion as well as pain.

Rask did not complain or fall behind even as the sun rose and began to sink. His expression spoke of fortitude and a hidden impetus. Perhaps, in time, he would ask Rask what compelled him, but not now. Now was the chase; now was the scent of blood on the air.

That oppressive atmosphere of slaughter and death grew as the sun set. Though they did not see the army, they saw its shadow upon the land – houses smoldering, land churned, corpses splayed in forgotten crevices.

The sun gazed red and hot at their backs as they came upon the valley. Within was arrayed the army of Margruxks, their shadows stretching downward toward it, black echoes of what was to come.

Smoke and fire filled the camp, the sound of metal and laughter, and the stench of thousands of unwashed men.

Zorsam paused his pursuit and stared down at the multitude of enemies. Rask stumbled to his side, breathing heavily and ready to collapse.

"I cannot slay them all. Margruxks is the one I will slay."

"Well," Rask said when he had breath. "See dat tent out der by de river on de ot'er side. It bears de royal seal. P'haps we kin finds him dere."

"Yes. It shall be finished quickly."

They waited until the red sun had extinguished itself and then slipped down into the valley. They moved in the shadows, Rask as soundless as Zorsam, along the edge of camp, making their way quickly toward the river. "You will wait here," he told Rask as they approached. The guards had been careless so far, sure of their own safety.

"I kin help you."

"Wait and watch. I will return."

The Great One had sent him Rask, but he did not know the reason. Zorsam knew *his* purpose was vengeance. He had emerged from his bestial state and witnessed the trail of atrocities that followed Margruxks. Margruxks deserved to die and Zorsam would enjoy delivering the blow.

With cunning Zorsam made his way, keeping to the deepest shadows and slinking as not to disturb his prey. Men sated on violence and drink did not fear as a man alone in the dark might. They caroused and scanned the horizon for armies they knew would not come. Zorsam slid beneath their gaze, silent, focused, a snake in the grass, until he reached the royal tent. It lay fat and bloated like a rotting carcass. He cut a slit in the back and crept inside.

Within, candles cast a dim and flickering light over a great bed arrayed in purple silk. Upon the bed lay a woman. Zorsam stepped closer. He recognized the face – Asundi. She was asleep now as she had been in Death's Lair and just as beautiful. Zorsam put out his hand to touch her raven hair but did not, as if it were the spikes of a porcupine or the stinger of a wasp. He dared not touch her. Not until his mission was complete and his people had regained the peace Margruxks had stolen from them. In his heart, the gentleness her beauty had sparked grew red and dark and turned to rage.

A voice emerged from the dimness behind him. "This is what you simple folk do not understand. You have come here to – what? Free her? Kill me? How simple-minded."

Zorsam turned and drew his sword, crouching down, alert.

"Manrix demands sacrifices in exchange for his favor. So, I deliver them. Exquisite gifts. That husk of girl is his. And will you prevent me?"

"Come and see what fate the Great One has for you, Margruxks!"

"I do not heed the words of savages. I have guards enough to deal with you. But it will be some pleasure seeing how easily you are thwarted."

Zorsam searched the tent with keen eyes, but he could not distinguish the form of Margruxks among the shadows. A premonition caused him to turn, and he saw a great cord of darkness wrapping itself about Asundi's slender body. Zorsam grabbed at the cord, but it was as smoke in his grasp, cold and oily. It began to pull her away. He reached out for her, to draw her back, but his fingers slipped, and he could find no grip on her.

"She will be devoured," Margruxks said. "Your people will be devoured, one by one, by sun and blood and fire."

Asundi was gone, taken beyond Zorsam's sight by sorcery he did not understand. He growled and paced forward into the tent, searching, prowling.

"It is time for you to die," Margruxks said.

"I know Death," Zorsam snarled. "I will give introductions."

CHAPTER 7: The Brothers' Wrath

A horn sounded outside the tent. Men rushed in, armored and armed, surrounding him. Zorsam swung his sword to ward them off, lancing out at those who dared step near. He howled at Margruxks' cowardice.

"Where are you?" Zorsam shouted. "Let us face each other!"

Two of the men ran at him from behind. He twisted quickly and with a powerful stroke removed their heads from their bodies. They fell to the ground in a heap, staining the already red carpet.

A third man felt Zorsam's sword in his belly. Zorsam removed the sword and spun, smashing his hilt against the skull of a fourth. These men attacked with abandon; they had no skill. Zorsam grabbed the fourth man as he stumbled back and flung him into a group of three moving forward together.

Candles fell to the ground in the struggle. Zorsam met the next man with strikes from his sword as flames licked the carpet and tent. He seized one of the fallen soldiers by the ankle and swung him in a wide circle, widening the noose of men attempting to close in on him again. He released the man, who flew against a support pole, cracking it. The roof sagged in Zorsam's corner.

Zorsam roared, arms thrown back, as the fire climbed higher, showering its bloody light upon the enemies struggling to their feet.

Something barreled into Zorsam from behind, hurling him forward with the force of a battering ram. He struck the tent wall and ripped through the flame-soaked skins before colliding with the ground and skidding across the rough rock. He rolled from his attacker and stood, his sword lost somewhere on the ground. Blood trickled from wounds cut by the rock.

A man stood broad and strong against the now flaming tent, waiting for Zorsam to face him. His eyes flared orange as Zorsam looked and the fires behind him rose, emanating a wave of intense heat. Zorsam covered his face from the blast and stepped back. When he looked again, serpents of fire slithered their way toward the man, collecting in a writhing ball above the man's hand. The entire structure behind him trembled and crumbled, leaving only a charred husk.

The ball of fire compressed and formed into a red-hot mace, which the man gripped firmly in his gauntleted hand. The glow of his weapon lit his broad, flat face and mane of red hair. His lips lifted into a grim smirk. In the weapon's light, Zorsam also glimpsed his sword, just out of reach.

A second warrior emerged from the dark behind him. He was smaller than the first. His armor was deep blue that shone like glass in the fire-mace's glare. His long hair and beard were white. His face was nearly identical to that of the first man. He stopped at the fire-wielder's side with a glance at the other, then examined Zorsam with cold eyes.

"This must be the beast who killed our brother," said the fiery one.

"I am not surprised, Zaduk," said the other. "Thar was young. He spoke too much. Let us not make the same mistake."

"Of course, Fria."

The blue warrior breathed in deeply and then exhaled, slivers of ice forming before him. With a wave of his hand, they darted toward Zorsam. Swift they were, piercing Zorsam in arm and chest like teeth. Zorsam dove for his sword. A fireball exploded upon the blade as Zorsam reached out. The blast burnt the flesh on his arm and forced him to roll away. He blinked, trying to find his vision in the night. He sensed an attacker behind him, so he turned as he stood, catching the man in cold armor and slamming him to the ground. Ducking, he avoided a fireball and, lunging forward, he smashed his fist into the red warrior's too-large face.

"Your sorcery shall not save you!" Zorsam shouted. "Fire and ice belong to the Great One, not to butchers and cowards!"

Fists clenched, he fell upon Zaduk with brute force, but Zaduk swung at him with his weapon of flame. Zorsam caught his wrist and smashed the warrior's hand against a rock, but the warrior would not yield. He breathed in, the flames swirling out of his hands and into his mouth. Then he exhaled streams of fire. Zorsam scrambled back, flames biting into his skin. Zaduk rose, spewing forth the fire of his soul and roasting Zorsam until he found his feet and escaped out of the range of Zaduk's breath.

Too late he sensed Fria behind him. A spear of ice descended upon him, cold and dark as it entered his back and exited his abdomen. It burned with the frost of deep winter.

Zorsam felt a veil cover his senses. He could hear the movement of camp and the whisper of flames. He could taste ash and blood. He saw Zaduk before him with his grim smile and Fria at his side, looking coldly at him. These things he understood as though watching from a distance.

For a moment, time seemed to slow, and he understood. He had felt this strange lapse before when fighting thunder lizards and sabercats. It was the knowledge of living compressed because Death was close. His cold fingers touched Zorsam now, not to aid or teach, but to collect if necessary.

This was the survival instinct waking, crying out, and Zorsam had felt it before. An animal fought to live because life was what it knew, what it *was*. But never before had Zorsam felt fear in this moment. For the first time, he was afraid to die – for he knew now death was not just a state, but a judgment.

He would stand, despite the pain. He would fight, despite the odds. He would find victory, somehow. He started to force his muscles…

A battle cry. It was small and shrill. Zaduk and Fria looked toward the sound. A small man rolled between them and landed in front of Zorsam. Rask tossed the sword he cradled to him.

With a swipe of his sword, Zorsam shattered the head of Fria's ice-spear, which stuck through his abdomen. Broken, the disenchanted weapon fell to the ground as water. As he stood, he turned and thrust his sword at Fria's chest. The warrior caught the blade between his palms, barely halting the momentum, so Zorsam punched him in the face. Behind Zorsam, Rask shouted insults at Zaduk.

Fria stumbled back. Zorsam grabbed him by the neck and shoved him into Zaduk, who had been distracted by Rask's taunts. The brothers fell to the ground. Zorsam roared, raised his sword over his head, and brought it down upon his enemies.

A wave of fire and ice blasted Zorsam, searing him, but he forced his sword down, muscles straining. The brothers held him back with a cross of elemental weapons, the freeze of the spear and the heat of the mace entwining with one another. Formed of the same dark magic, they strengthened each other and held back Zorsam's blade. The barbarian bared his teeth. His eyes shone with a storm's intensity, with Nature's own implacable force.

The brothers saw the expression and their grips began to slip. "What manner of man are you?" Fria asked.

"I am the Hunter and the Slayer, the Avenger's Wrath." Zorsam pressed with trembling muscles. "I am Zorsam!"

"Er... Zorsam," Rask said behind him, "dis bad time ta fight." The man touched his back. "We's gonna die if we don't run."

It was then Zorsam noticed the soldiers closing in. If he managed to subdue the brothers, the soldiers would have him; and if he turned to engage the soldiers, the brothers would begin their magical attacks once again.

He did not care, however. He would destroy them all. He was the messenger of Death. He was the sword thirsty for blood.

Rask patted him frantically. "We's gonna die. Dat what you wants?"

He had been saved from the well. He had been given personhood once more. Was it so he could die here? He burned to fight, ached to kill and slay all evil. He felt Rask's hand upon his sweat-drenched back.

He roared, unable to contain his rage, his frustration, and grabbed Rask in one arm, throwing him over his shoulder. Then he sprinted away into the night, away from the brothers and the soldiers… away from Margruxks and his camp, away…

CHAPTER 8: Wounds

Hot blood and sweat chilled beneath the wind of his passage. Burnt flesh and burning muscles darkened his body in pain. Within his chest something sat black and ugly.

Margruxks, the oppressor of his people, the slayer of virgins, the acolyte of the hungry god, still lived. His lackeys still lived, having attacked and injured him. He had faltered. He had turned and run. He was a broken sword, a wounded animal, a bloodied judge.

In his heart he felt shame, and it made him heavy. It made him tremble.

Zorsam continued into the night, into the darkness that enveloped him. If they pursued, he did not hear them, and Rask did not tell him. The small man was silent except for grunts that spoke of his uneasy position.

Soon Zorsam felt safety, and he hated it.

They came to the peak of a hill at the edge of a valley where the grass was thick and soft. Beyond was a dell where ancient trees muttered together. Zorsam descended among the trees, the deep calm of night and sanctuary closing about him as he entered beneath their high and wise branches. He stumbled and stood again and stumbled. He fell to his knees and Rask rolled off.

What was the use of standing again? Zorsam collapsed upon the grass and lay there, meditating upon his wounds and the language of pain.

Nothing moved except for Rask, who was as quiet as a rat. "You's alright?"

Zorsam did not answer. He listened to the pain and heard the meaning behind its strange speech. It spoke the language of beasts, and yet when he listened, he heard something beneath, something above and within, that seemed to him a whispering of the Great One.

***

Warmth hummed in his ears, singing in its kind way. Zorsam opened his eyes. The sun was rising, the sky red in rebirth. The trees met it with the green of life, the leaves rustling beneath the wind's caress. Beneath his head was a stone, cool and hard and solid.

The pain murmured like water in the distance, like cool refreshment sought upon a journey. The deeper ache within, the shame, sat old and rotten like a mushroom; not so heavy as before but still vile and alien.

He smelled ointment upon his skin. Dark green wads of leaves covered his wounds. He sat up and leaned against the smooth bark of a tree. Rask dozed nearby, curled like a child between two exposed roots.

"Rask," Zorsam called.

The little man's eyes shot open and he scrambled to a sitting position. "I apologize. I's keepin' watch. I musta fallen asleep."

"You did this?" Zorsam nodded to the poultice.

"You don't mind, do you? It was hard ta see in de dark like dat, but I knows you's hurt."

"What is it?"

"De lotion taken from de vera plant. It cools de burns. De leaves in yer wounds comes from de icemint tree. By chewin' and waddin' dem, dey soof cuts an' helps healin'. Lots o' dem bof grow in dis forest."

Zorsam nodded. "It is good the Great One sent you to me."

Rask's round face split in half as he smiled. "I just dids what I could."

Zorsam looked again at this small man. Zorsam walked in strength and breathed the vapors of conflict. By Death's commission, his sword wrought vengeance and his victory secured justice. Rask was not the predator, but neither was he merely prey.

"Did you finds Margruxks?"

"He spoke but he did not reveal himself. He took Asundi and sent those two sorcerers in his place."

"Asoondi? Who dat?"

"She is the princess of my people. Margruxks plans to sacrifice her to his god."

"A princess, eh? I's never seen no princess."

38

"She is alluring, like a trap ready to close. She was the first other I saw upon understanding. She lies as if dead, but when I looked upon her, I first realized what mankind is. He is not formed as one, but as two."

Rask whistled. "You's in love."

Zorsam did not comprehend the word, for in his memories, the word brought forth images of his mother. "It is not that. It is revelation from the Great One. She was the one given to me when the act of vengeance was declared." He mused upon the words. "I was charged not simply to destroy. I am to protect."

Rask nodded sagely. "Protect yer woman. I understands."

Zorsam felt the word "your" as a sudden constriction. "I will protect her. I will shield her and she will be safe. This I declare." Rask looked at him with an expression of pity, and Zorsam turned away. "Do not mock me!"

"I's not mockin'! I's listenin'!"

For a time, Rask remained silent, and Zorsam stood and tested his limbs. His abdominal wound was tender but healing; the ice spear seemed more dangerous in battle than recovery. He ached and burned as he moved his arms and legs, testing their strength, but it was pain he could ingest, pain he could listen to and command. He felt the weakness in his muscles, though, that only rest could eliminate as after a fever. If he called upon the fullness of his abilities, he would fail.

"Is she be'tiful?" Rask asked.

Zorsam thought of the stars in the crisp winter air and how he felt an expanse of peace beneath them. He thought of the leopard, sleek and skillful, stalking through the forest, and of the power she contained within her tight-knit body. He thought of the spider's web clothed in dew, intricate and fragile, a kingdom and a wisp. And he remembered Asundi's raven hair, her proud and royal face, the strong, unbowed neck, the mystery of those closed eyes.

"Yes."

"Dat's good." Rask looked into the canopy of golden morning. "I's a farmer, didja know? I likes the rough dirt in my hands an' sweat on de brow. Honest, hard-workin' sweat, not dis runnin' from de enemy drenchin'." Rask shut his mouth and began to stand. "You wants to go, I suppose?"

"Not yet."

He felt in the calm, cool air a hesitation. It may have been the dark stain of shame upon his conscience. It may have been the lingering image of Asundi upon his heart. It may have been the expectation in the pauses of Rask's speech.

Zorsam had spent many days in silence, stalking and watching, and he sensed now he should pause. He was impatient, and yet experience had taught him that to pounce, one must be ready.

He sat, listening to the silence and the deep, silent murmurs beneath. Had the Great One spoken to him in such ways even in his bestial days?

"Tell me about yourself, Rask," he said after a time. That was what was unspoken between them, the need of Rask to reveal and the necessity of Zorsam to listen. "Who were you?"

Rask folded his legs beneath himself and, a smile upon his face, began to talk eagerly.

"Like I saids, I just a farmer in Deet. No one dought much o' me. 'Dat's just Rask de Rat.' I's small, as you sees, an' workin' in de dirt don't makes you nobil'ty. One day I was in de market lookin' for seed for de next season. My bag was heavy an' I's in a hurry. I's always scurryin' 'round, dat's why dey call me Rat. I tripped. No one helped poor Rask, didn't expect no one, but der she was. She sold flowers on de corner an' she stooped down ta help.

"She was be'tiful, Zorsam. Hair red as apple, eyes green as crop. I's had trouble lookin' at what I were doin', you know? I ain't seen yer Asoondi, but it don't matter. I's seen *her*.

"'You's hurt?' she asked. Told her I'd be fine, starin' at her and scrabblin' 'round for my seeds like a blind man. Den she gave me a firerose just ta put a smile on my face. Dose dings only bloom fer a day. Dey's expensive. What could I do? I said dank you. I couldn't stop dinkin' 'bout her afta' dat. Plowin' an' plantin', all I could dink about was her. I'd heard men'd climb mountains an' fight beasts for der woman, and dat's when I understood. I dought I could maybe even be brave enough ta talk ta her again.

"So, I headed back to town and I hunted her down an' I asks her, 'What will it take ta make you my wife?' She don't believe me, but I'm serious. I asks her again, an' she smiles again. I kin't hardly stand it. 'Climb de Burnin' Mountain,' she says, 'and bring me a bouquet o' fireroses.'

"She was jokin'. I seen it in her face. But de next day I climbed dat mountain. Didn't pack nufin'. Just started walkin'. I nearly died, I did. An' once I had dem flowers, I had ta get dem to her before sundown or dey'd start wiltin'. Last bloody ray of de sun I hand dem ta her. She yelled at me good fer doin' someding so stupid. Few months later, she's my wife."

40

Zorsam considered his words. "I asked who you were. I did not ask about your mate."

Rask looked away. "De army o' Glaur came afta' dat. My prince, man from my own village, Prince Zarn of Garr, surrendered de city when Margruxks offered ta make him a general instead o' killin' him. Margruxks captured all de young women ta be sacrificed ta Manrix. De last I saw my wife, she was cryin' fer help as de lightnin' man took her from me. I tried ta save her, but I couldn't." Rask grew stiff and he seemed very small. "I heard her screams from de temple." Rask stood, his back to him. "Dat's who I am. A rat dat found his own, den lost her."

He walked away, hiding from Zorsam an emotion dreadful and lonely. It spoke terrible words, full of vast expanses of empty blackness. He had never felt another's pain before. He found that it pierced as deeply as his own, and in the piercing, he found a brotherhood.

Zorsam sat stunned by the ache in his chest, as something inexpressible in his newfound language beat against him. He stood, threw back his arms and roared. He gave sound to the shame of his failures, to the injustice of women taken and men dead, to the woman who had been Rask's and now was no more, and to the doomed princess who waited for Zorsam.

He gave sound to the pain of humiliation, as he stepped down from his place as Avenger to stand among those who had suffered. He roared because, like a beast, he had no grasp of the meaning of suffering and could not give it a name.

Rask touched his arm. "Quiet. You don't wants Margruxks findin' us."

Zorsam looked upon the little man and saw him anew. "You are a great man, Rask, to bear so heavy a weight."

"I's nufin'. Ain't no one but suffers someding."

"I will share your pain. We will bear it together."

Rask looked up at him. He said nothing, but there were things that needed no words.

"I am the Great One's hammer, Rask, but I think he sent you to me so that I might be wielded well. The Great One detests Manrix and his sacrifices. I, too, detest them. But, perhaps, I cannot bear the burden for vengeance alone."

"I followed Margruxks," Rask said solemnly. "His blood for hers. Livin' by de leftovers o' de dead, chasin' afta' him. Me, de Rat, huntin' a wolf."

"Do not worry, my friend," said Zorsam, putting his meaty hand on Rask's bony shoulder. "Together, we will catch the wolf."

CHAPTER 9: Princess of the Dangray

By midday, Zorsam felt health return to his limbs and spirit. "It is time to move."

Rask eyed him doubtfully, but he removed the leaves from Zorsam's wounds, checking them. "You heals quick," he muttered.

Rask had already readied more poultice for future use and after gathering some fruit and roots for food, he too was ready to go. Zorsam watched the little man scurry to and fro, preparing, and he laughed, seeing his energy.

"You are finally ready?" Zorsam asked jovially.

"Yea."

"Then we run."

Out from beneath the trees they ran, out from the thick grass and cool shade into the heat of the unblinking sun. Toward the camp they returned with swift feet, Rask keeping pace with his short legs, Zorsam straining forward with the stride of a gazelle.

Soon, they reached the valley where Margruxks had camped the night before. Smoldering fires and trampled grass remained. The scent of thousands of dirt and blood-stained men lingered. Zorsam stood upon the edge of the valley, head held high, eyes scanning the far distance. He caught sign of the trail and he knew in his heart the way he must go.

Down the valley slope they went, through the churned and beaten grass, across the cool river, splashing. They continued, their clothes drying beneath the heavy gaze of the sun and the wind of their passing.

The army had moved quickly. That much was evident, and Zorsam had lost most of a day. Still, he ran with the speed of single-minded determination, and

Rask matched him stride for stride. East they traveled, the reddening sun beating back and neck as it set behind them.

Zorsam had tracked stampedes that left less destruction. Margruxks trampled and tore the land, furrowing it beneath the hard boots of murderers and the iron-shod wheels of the slave wagons. The land cried out. Zorsam could hear it, for he had long lived in the dirt like a beast.

The land baked beneath the sun, then fell to charcoal and ash. Night consumed the sky and spread its cloak across the earth. He could hear the marching army, still moving, a thunder of metal and men. He was almost upon them. But his body spoke of its weakness. He was not yet ready to face Margruxks again. The iron of his body was not yet repaired.

They were in foothills now, and he climbed among the rocks, looking for a place to spend the night. Rask saw the cave first, and together they entered. They found bones within, along with clothes and broken armor. The tomb had been ransacked. The stench of death remained.

"They have been here already," Zorsam said. "They will not return tonight."

Rask looked about the small space with an uneasy air. "Dis is what I dids – wif Gleen."

"You do so no longer, and you were in need." Zorsam sat heavily. "I am tired."

"I take de first watch. You needs yer rest."

A powerful weariness pressed upon Zorsam, so he did not argue. Pushing away the debris, he spread himself out upon the cold, hard floor of the tomb. His eyes fell shut and he surrendered to the dark claw of sleep.

***

Zorsam stood in fog that burnt his skin like ice. He could see neither ground nor ceiling, wall nor light, and yet he saw and stood and was confined.

"Zorsam!"

The voice beckoned him. It was not Death's voice. He did not recognize it and yet he listened and knew it to be familiar. It sang to him and it beseeched him.

"Zorsam!"

He moved through the fog and suffered its sting. He pressed forward toward the voice that came from nowhere and led him toward it.

43

"Zorsam!"

It was a cry for help. He ran through the veil of ice, ran through a space in which he could not navigate, sensing a form before him, reaching out for him. It lifted its arm and outstretched its hand.

Zorsam took the hand…

***

Three giggling girls chase after a tree rat. Their hair is dark silk, their eyes blue, and they run on feet calloused and dirt-stained. Their animal pelt dresses flutter as they run. The tallest of the three wears a headband with purple roses. The tree rat darts through the grass and up the trunk of a tree, into the leaves.

The smallest of the girls stamps her foot. The second crosses her arms and crinkles her nose. But the third strokes her chin, as she has seen her mother do, and looks about for some answer. She sees an apple on the ground and smiles. Grabbing it, she watches the leaves above. She sees a patch rustle and throws the apple. The tree rat falls to the ground. It lands on its feet, glances at the girls, and twitches its bushy tail before scampering away.

"Get him!" commands the purple-flowered girl.

The girls run off, but the purple-flowered girl feels a blow. She turns and sees an apple on the ground. She stretches her long, bronze arms behind her to rub the sore spot as she searches, finding no one. With a spasm of childish anger, she hurls the apple at the tree.

She turns to join her friends and receives another blow to the back. She growls and squats down defensively as she retrieves the new apple. She clutches it till it bruises.

A small boy wearing only a loincloth drops from the tree, laughing.

"Zorsam!" she chides, sounding like her mother. She throws the apple at him, but the boy catches it and bites a chunk of flesh from it.

The girl stomps toward him, swinging her fists, but he intercepts the blows, dropping the apple. He spins her around and slams her against the trunk of the tree. The girl groans in pain, but Zorsam laughs and dances as the men do when they return home with their prey.

The girl turns away as tears fill her eyes. The boy steps forward. "Asundi?"

She turns again, shoves him with both hands, and laughs as he stumbles to his back. He glares at her.

44

"Come get me!" she cries as she runs. The land runs with her and the sky spins and night falls.

Men dance around the fire as the leaders of the tribe watch. The chieftain is crowned with a lion's mane, the chieftess with a rosebush circlet. Asundi sits on the chieftain's lap.

The boy catches her eye from the other side of the fire. He dances with his mother, who is with child. Asundi wiggles in her father's lap, but his grip is firm. She climbs to his shoulders and whispers in his ear. He smiles approvingly, and Asundi's face glows. She jumps to the ground.

A trumpet roars. Hooves and shouts force the music to silence, and the dancers stand unmoving. Asundi stops amid the crowd, afraid.

The trumpet roars again, closer now. Riders appear at the edge of the firelight and encircle those celebrating. Asundi's father snatches her from the ground and runs as battle erupts around her. A masked rider on a black horse raises his sword, and one of her father's warriors charges the skull-faced rider. With a flash, the warrior falls to the ground, limp and wet and red.

The girl covers her eyes and screams.

Then her father is thrusting her to her mother's arms, and she wails, fighting to cling to him. Her mother holds her tight. Huts burn and waves of heat pummel her. Her father brings a horse and she is lifted onto it to sit pressed close to her mother. Her father kisses her and he speaks to her and then he is gone and the horse is galloping away from the fires and fallen men, into the dark.

Asundi tries to look back. She sees the skull-faced man, his sword bright in the firelight. Shadows rush around him. Her mother moves and she cannot see. She cries out, wordless and angry, straining to see again. She catches another glimpse. She sees her father's face, turning toward her one last time as the skull-faced man's sword strikes him. The face flies through the air, illuminated for a moment, and then lands somewhere in the night.

The wails do not seem her own, but those of another girl, far older.

Asundi jumps off the horse and begins to run. Night becomes day. Her toes dig into the ground for extra speed. Her muscular legs strain forward. Sweat drips down her bare, bronze abdomen. Her bare arms pump as she pushes more speed from her body. Her hair flies behind her. She skids to a stop and looks down into the ravine. She is grown and beautiful and strong.

Panting, she searches for signs of life. There is fear in her eyes, a quiver that betrays her strength. A shout echoes out from behind. She draws her dagger and turns to the Glaur soldiers pursuing her. She has only seconds before they find her.

"Princess!"

The voice comes from below. Upon a ledge stands a warrior smeared with war paint. He motions to her. She sheaths her dagger and jumps down to him. He catches her and presses her against the wall of the ravine. They still their breathing and wait.

Armor rattles above them, and pebbles scatter down. "She's escaped!" the commander says. "Double back. We'll find her."

The sounds of men fade, but still they wait, letting the silence reach full measure. Finally, the warrior climbs the rock wall, pulling himself over the jutting precipice. Asundi follows, allowing the warrior to aid her.

"I thought I had lost you, Shamgar," she says, dusting herself off.

"My apologies, Princess." Shamgar bows slightly. "Now, we must find the other warriors and return to camp by nightfall."

With stealth, they move through the wilderness until they reach camp. Just outside the perimeter of low hills, Asundi takes a headband from a pouch on her skirt and puts it on. Purple petals crown her head. Then they enter through the hidden break in the rocks to where men and women work at small tasks. There is a hesitation as she walks among them. Hands still for a moment. Eyes look to her.

Asundi smiles at them, weakness pushed back, exhaustion hidden in the corner of her eyes. One little girl waves at her shyly.

A man with thinning hair and a gray beard stands at the mouth of the cave. He is worn and thin, and his face is grim.

"What is it, Hansi?" Asundi asks.

"Come inside."

She follows him, Shamgar leaving her side to attend to other duties.

A few torches fill the interior with strange light and smoke. Handcrafted tables, beds, and chairs fill the enclosure. Hansi leads Asundi to one of the tables.

"Manoah has been captured," he says.

Asundi face becomes stone. "When?"

"Six months ago. Word just reached us, after you went on the hunt with Shamgar."

She sits heavily. "He was the last of our nobles. What of his clan?"

46

"Captured or killed. We are now the last of the free peoples."

Asundi covers her face with her hands. Silent tears are on her cheeks. "Help us, O Great One," she whispers.

"Princess, we have no more options. We must surrender to Glaur or die."

She stands, pushing the chair back and onto the ground. "We are the Dangray. We bow to none but the Great One!"———

"He is dead!" snaps Hansi. "He was wounded the night Glaur raided our village all those years ago, and he has been dying ever since. You have been our one hope, the symbol of our heritage, yet you risk your life hunting. This is over. We have lost."

"I am no hope." Asundi rights the chair and sits again. "I hunt to learn the warrior's way. I will fight with my people until the Great One relents and acts. He will hear our prayers and he will save us."

"You are no chieftain. When your mother died, you told me you did not want the burden of these people. Marry and let another take your place. Shamgar is a worthy suitor and a fine warrior."

Asundi turns from Hansi, pain in her expression. "I vowed never to marry until my people were free from Margruxks and his enslavement. I will not enjoy such a union until my people are able to celebrate with me."

Hansi walks around the table and lowers himself, so that he is face to face with the princess. "And while you sit here, our people slave in the work camps, erecting monuments to Manrix and his bloody appetite. Should we not join them? We will die when Glaur comes, and they *will* come. Should we not surrender instead, so that we may live a little longer and die among our people?"

Asundi meets his gaze. "The Great One will not remain silent for much longer. Until he acts, we refuse to bow our knee to Margruxks and his so-called god. Glaur will not devour us. We will not bow. Ever. I will die before then."

"And what of us?"

A shiver runs through Asundi's frame. "If you follow me, you follow me."

Hansi stands. "You are a fool."

Asundi holds herself still as he exits the cave. Then she lays her face upon the table and begins to weep.

She cuts her sorrow short. Outside, horse hooves, swords, and shouts clatter together. She looks toward the cave's entrance with a tear-drenched face. A man rushes into the room, blocking the view. She jumps to her feet, her dagger in hand.

ZORSAM AND THE GOD WHO DEVOURS

It is Shamgar.

"Glaur has found us." He grabs her arm. "You must run."

Through the cave's entrance they flee. The cacophony of battle envelopes her as she enters the darkening day. Black warhorses gallop through the camp, Dangray warriors engage with Glaur soldiers, and she strides through the conflict, moving low and quick, dagger ready to strike.

A thunderbolt strikes the ground before her. The force of the blast knocks her off her feet. Shamgar is still standing, and he guards her from the unseen enemy with his stave.

She gains her feet. The man is there, sparks dancing across his heavy armor. He holds his monstrous sword loosely in his hand. His eyes flare with blue fire. "This is the princess, then? I did not know such beauty existed among your filthy race."

Shamgar charges. With a flick of his hand, lightning shoots forth from the enemy's palm. It strikes Shamgar in the chest and he flies through the air, past Asundi. He lands hard, but he still breathes. Asundi takes a defensive stance.

Two soldiers appear at the armored man's side. "Take her," he orders.

She slashes the first across his throat, spraying blood, but the second lands a fist on her mouth. Blood runs down her chin. He follows with a blow to her abdomen and another to her side, but she keeps her feet and spies her opening. With a quick jab, she stabs the soldier through a gap in his armor. As he steps back in pain, she scoops up a rock, lunges forward, and smashes it against his helmet.

As the soldier drops, Asundi turns to face the man of lightning.

Electricity runs through her. She falls to her knees, muscles convulsing in the constant charge. She smells the faint aroma of burnt skin.

"You little harlot." The armored man approaches, playing with threads of electricity balled in his hands like a woman unraveling tangled yarn. "You couldn't just surrender, could you?" With sudden anger he backhands her, and she hits the ground. "Your tribe's been a thorn in my lord's side for twenty years."

He kicks her in the ribs. She cannot fight back. She cannot even scream. The man pulls her to her feet by her shirt, electricity swirling in his free hand. "Now you will be devoured like all the others."

"Unhand her, Thar!"

The armored man lowers his fist. The horror from her past, the man in the skull mask, approaches.

Thar throws Asundi to the ground and she groans. She clings to consciousness.

"She is the last of the Dangray's royalty," Thar says. "We should kill her here and be done with it."

"She is needed," the skull replies.

"Manrix demands blood!"

"He will have it, in time."

Thar points an accusatory finger at the masked man. "Who are you to decide the will of the God Who Devours?"

The masked man grabs Thar by the throat. "I am Margruxks, conquering king of Glaur and favored son of the Devourer. My word is absolute. You will obey. Do not forget it was *I* who brought you and your brothers to Manrix. Without me, you would have been another dead cutthroat in Cimmara. You owe me your allegiance and your life!"

He releases Thar, who falls to the ground, coughing. "Now, bring the girl. I have plans for her."

***

Zorsam awoke with a start. His limbs were cold with sweat and he sat up, panting. After a moment, he stood, took hold of his sword, and kicked Rask awake. The first touch of sun was lighting the night.

"What's happenin'?" Rask asked, rubbing his ribs.

"We move."

"We should eat someding—"

"Now."

"What's happened?"

"Come. Margruxks must die."

CHAPTER 10: The God Who Devours

That day they crossed the wastes of Glaur in pursuit of Margruxks and his army. Zorsam moved with boundless energy born of fury. His vision drove him forward. The events seemed to him as vivid as if he had witnessed them in the flesh. He knew his people; he understood Asundi and longed for her. He pressed forward like wind through the crack, like an arrow toward the target, like the burning sun toward the horizon of its night.

Rask called for Zorsam to slow. He choked for breath and asked for a moment's rest. The moment was too long, a veritable eternity. Zorsam growled and paced and charged forward as soon as Rask could stand straight.

He was wild, feral. He felt it and he knew it and he did not restrain it.

They came to a pass between two spires of rock. A city lay below, its long stone walls stained and cracked and shattered, its streets filled with slow streams of people. In its center rose a temple of earth and stone and extravagance. The city was red with the evening light. The day had passed in a blink. It did not matter. Zorsam trembled in body. He had reached his adversary. The army could be seen encamped outside the walls.

"What is this place?"

"De city o' Zorah," Rask gasped. He sat and tried to recover himself. "I hear its walls were be'tiful an' invincible. 'Til dey came, dat is. It were one o' de first places conquered."

Zorsam nodded and began to descend.

"Where you's goin'?" Rask called irritably, getting to his feet.

"To Margruxks."

"You plans ta fight de whole army? You's tough but you knows you's not dat tough."

The memory of his shame cooled his fever for a moment. "What does the Rat say?"

Rask took a few more breaths to compose himself. "A bit o' sneakin's called fer. Dey's camped by de west gate. We takes de long way 'round an' takes de norf gate. Dey never sees us come in, den we finds Margruxks and de girl."

Zorsam scanned the army. His instincts told him to press forward, sword swinging. His mind and experience told him to listen to the little man.

"Lead the way."

***

Merchants called out among the small crowd, hawking fruit, trinkets, animals, slaves. The smell of manure and sweat hung heavy in the air. Men walked wearily through the streets.

One merchant extended a foul-smelling piece of meat in front of Zorsam's face as he passed. "Want some lizard on a stick? Good stuff. Keep you strong."

Zorsam walked past without response. Two armored guards stood at the corner, and he approached them as Rask regretfully left the meat behind.

"Where is Margruxks?" Zorsam demanded.

"Who's asking?"

"I am Zorsam. I have a message for the king."

The guards looked at one another. "He's probably at Manrix's temple."

"We go," he told Rask.

The small man nodded and led Zorsam through the labyrinthine streets that tangled their way to the center of the city like roots snaking to the trunk of a tree. Through narrow alleys that stank of excrement and wider avenues of fractured paving stone they carefully made their way until the buildings disappeared, and the courtyard of the temple opened before them.

The temple pierced the sky, its windows blinded by wooden shutters, its eaves haunted by winged demons of stone. Six pillars supported the portico roof, and at its end, massive crimson doors opened into the dark maw of the sanctuary. Glaur soldiers swarmed the entrance.

"Dis temple once dedicated ta god named de Ancient o' Days, I dink. P'haps yer Great One knows him."

Zorsam reached for his sword as he stepped forward. He turned back when Rask did not follow. The little man just shook his head.

"I grow tired of skulking like a rat," Zorsam growled.

"You kin't grow tired dead," Rask said. "Follow me."

Rask led Zorsam back into the surrounding streets and around to the temple's north side until they were opposite the portico entrance. The buildings here, well-built homes, were hung with talismans and strange symbols.

"Homes of de priests, probly," Rask explained, seeing Zorsam's look. "Now just walk like you belongs here." Rask glanced at Zorsam. "As much as you kins."

The open area was much narrower here, with no guards at the moment and only a few townspeople within earshot. They reached the temple and stopped beneath one of the shuttered windows. "Pry it open," Rask said, scanning the area. "Now."

Zorsam jabbed his sword between the shutters. With one quick yank, it ripped off. Rask climbed through, motioning Zorsam to follow.

Candlelight and incense filled the large room. In its center, dimly lit, was a bowl-like pool. Within was not water but flesh. The naked bodies of men and women entwined with one another, their soft groans rising like the moan of an injured animal. They moved sluggishly, as if drugged or drunk. They were not aware of Zorsam's presence, and he turned away in disgust. This was a thing of beasts and perversion.

Rask covered his eyes with his hands. "Dis was de pool for purification, I bet. Now—"

"The master shapes his men. Come."

"Ain't you gonnas do some avengin'? Dose—"

"Margruxks first."

He passed through the door into the temple sanctuary. Columns supported the high ceiling, and gold reflected the hundreds of candles set along the perimeter of the sacred circle. Smoke drifted darkly above the tiled floor where the refuse of relics and shattered remains of an altar littered the ground. In the center of the destruction towered a demon-wolf, jaws wide with teeth, claws out as it reared up on hind legs, almost manlike. The ebony stone of the idol shone in the flickering light of the candles, giving movement to its dark pelt and menace to the merciless orbs of its eyes.

The tile before it was wet, and Zorsam smelled the tang of blood. A decrepit priest, cowled in a black robe, recited prayers before the idol in a blacker tongue. Behind him, a dozen worshippers lay prostrate, moaning.

Zorsam gripped his sword. He had told Rask he would seek Margruxks first for vengeance, even as the perversion of prostitution enraged him. Here, before this unholy ceremony, he found the same spirit of prostitution in their dark worship. Zorsam had spoken with Death, and in that encounter been shown only a glimpse of the Great One. That glimpse was enough to show him the depth of corruption in this room. It was to see the sun and sing that the world might burn and be purified.

He stepped forward to slay these men, to destroy this place, but at that moment a door beyond opened, spilling light into the dark convocation, and a voice called, "Clear out!"

The worshippers slipped away, and the priest turned toward the voice. Zorsam watched, too, Rask pulling him back into the shadow of the doorway. The voice belonged to a black-haired man, handsome and fierce, clad in red garments and gold armor. Upon the armor was the impression of a black wolf.

Behind the man walked Fria and Zaduk, and between them they carried a litter covered with thick cloth.

The priest bowed to the dark-haired man. "My Lord Margruxks."

Zorsam tensed. The skull-masked man in his vision, the one he had been sent to destroy, stood across the room from him. He burned. This man had slaughtered his people and many others, he had demolished the old ways and mocked the Great One, he had seized Asundi. Rask's hand touched his trembling arm, and he restrained his wrath. The Brothers were there beside Margruxks. If he confronted the three in haste, he would fail.

"Scragg, you vermin," answered Margruxks.

"How may I serve your Lordship?" The priest removed his hood, revealing a bald, pale head.

"I have arrived with my offering." Margruxks pulled back the litter's covering, revealing Asundi's unconscious form.

The priest cooed, hobbling forward. "She is a beautiful one."

Margruxks seized Scragg's wrist, eliciting a cry of pain. "She is not destined for your whorehouse. She shall feed Manrix's appetite, not yours."

"Your men have brought many virgins for sacrifice. What's special about this one?"

Margruxks relinquished his grip. "She is the tribal princess of the Dangray, who worship Manrix's enemy, whom they call the Great One. I offer her to Manrix in exchange for a portion of his power."

"Ah. The Ritual of Deity."

"Yes, as you explained to me long ago. It is time, and she is the one."

Scragg wandered around the altar of the demon wolf, considering. "The power granted you through ordinary sacrifice of lives is not enough for you, then. You desire godhood."

"You saw it in me when we first met. My reign will be eternal, my kingdom indomitable. I will live and I will rule, and the world shall bow before me." Margruxks stepped forward. "Do you hesitate?"

"No, of course not, my Lord."

"Then begin the ritual."

Scragg shook his head, back turned toward Margruxks. "I cannot," he croaked.

"Why?"

"The ritual calls for a virgin of enemy royal blood, one without blemish, to be sacrificed in a temple wholly consecrated to the Great Devourer Manrix." Scragg returned to Asundi's side, gazing down hungrily, but he kept his hands folded before him. "This woman is still healing from blows inflicted, I assume, by your men. This is minor. This temple, however, is insufficient for the rite. This place has been absorbed by Manrix, but it is not consecrated to him. We must perform the ceremony at the Tower Xalthu."

"It shall be done," said Margruxks.

"It shall *not*," declared Zorsam, breaking forth from the shadows. His sword was in his hand and his face bore the savagery of the lion. He roared as he charged.

Margruxks showed no surprise and no fear but looked at Zorsam with curiosity. The Brothers, however, moved forward.

Ice solidified suddenly around Zorsam's legs. He broke through the first layer, but he stumbled as it reformed. He hit the ground, his sword clattering away. As Zorsam kicked free of the ice, Zaduk rammed his boot into Zorsam's back. Zorsam bucked and nearly escaped before Fria joined his brother and pressed Zorsam to the floor.

Margruxks crouched down to looked at him. "You Dangray are resilient."

The ice was thickening on his legs, numbing him. "You will die for killing my people! I have been sent to avenge them and to deal the justice of the Great One."

"I thought, perhaps, you had come for the princess," Margruxks said. "You seem unsuited to such foolish motivation. Vengeance, however, that I understand." He grabbed Zorsam's hair and pulled the barbarian's head back, though he strained against it. "You are wilder than even the rest of your people. You stink of caves and pits. You bare your teeth madly, like an injured dog. You do not even understand the forces at work here. I have enslaved your people, and I will sacrifice your princess. Then even Death shall obey me."

"Death listens to none but the Great One, and I listen to Death."

Margruxks released Zorsam's hair; his face hit the floor hard.

Margruxks stood. "Kill him."

Zorsam felt a tongue of fire tickle his neck. "With pleasure," said Zaduk.

But he suddenly fell forward into his brother with a shrill cry. With the momentary release of pressure, Zorsam reached out and managed to grab his sword. With two quick strikes, he shattered the ice on his legs and found his feet, wavering a little on his numb limbs.

He saw now what had distracted the brothers. Rask was on Zaduk's back, tightening his belt around the fire warrior's neck. Fria was just finding his feet again. Zorsam lunged at Margruxks, but the king drew his sword and parried smoothly. Zorsam stepped back, then quickly took another step, sensing Fria's swing. The blade passed in front of him.

"Get the girl," Margruxks said, taking a fighting stance. "I'll handle the beast."

Rask screamed. Zorsam looked to find that Zaduk had tossed the little man off his back and was raising a fiery fist to strike him. Zorsam scooped up a piece of debris and hurled it at Zaduk. It smacked him in the head, knocking him sideways. Rask took the opportunity to scurry away.

Zorsam turned back to Margruxks, who studied him but did not strike. Fria had Asundi over his shoulder. Zaduk joined him.

"She is mine!" Zorsam declared.

"So, it is not merely vengeance," Margruxks said.

Zorsam leapt forward, bringing his sword down on the tyrant's head. His sword crashed against his foe's, and he leapt back to avoid the counterattack. None came.

"Fight me!"

"I do not stay my hand out of pity," said Margruxks. His piercing gaze looked at Zorsam and past the barbarian warrior, as if he did not see what was before him. His lips curved in a cruel smile. "I have other duties, more important than this, and my god has his own plans."

Zorsam glimpsed the form of the priest, pressed flat against the floor, crawling to Margruxks, and with two quick strides, caught him and pulled him up by his robe.

"Give me Asundi, or this man dies!"

Margruxks sheathed his sword. "We will meet again, beast. Scragg, give my regards to Manrix."

Zorsam threw the priest down, charging toward Margruxks. He slammed into a wall of ice that solidified before him. He hit with such force his vision went black as he fell back. Struggling against unconsciousness, he regained his feet. Through the wall he saw the distorted figure of Margruxks walking away. Fria was at his side, lingering.

Zorsam struck the ice with his sword. Chips flew into the air. He struck again, bellowing. His blade slashed the wall and dug narrow crevices, but it would not crack. He threw down his sword and pounded with his fists, his face pressed against the brutal cold. It burned him.

He turned at a sudden sound. Scragg was rising to his feet. Zorsam, chest heaving, soul afire with failure and wrath, picked up his sword and strode to the panicked priest.

"Manrix, save me!"

Zorsam hacked the old man to pieces with three incredible blows.

He turned to the idol. "What are you?" Zorsam demanded. "Nothing! You will grovel before the arm of the Great One!"

Zorsam wedged himself beneath the idol's jaws, placed his broad shoulders against the strangely warm metal, and pushed. His legs strained against the weight. He held his back firm as iron. With a roar, with a shuddering of rage, he pushed, and he thought of the blood upon his sword and of Margruxks upon it, and he pushed; his muscles burning, tearing, and he heaved with a final decisive act of will.

The idol cracked off its base, tilted beneath Zorsam's strength, and crashed upon the floor. The impact echoed through the sanctuary.

He stood, almost blind with single purpose. He looked upon his demolition. Rask cowered nearby, looking upon him with fear.

"I will crush everything," Zorsam declared. Manrix lay broken before him. "I am the Destroyer."

"My son."

The voice was ancient and deep. Zorsam looked upon the idol. Its eyes looked back at him.

"Vengeance is thine, my son," it whispered. "Let my fires be added to yours. Let my appetite be added to yours. Margruxks is mine. I shall give him to you. Asundi is mine. I shall give her to you. Your sword shall drink the blood of your enemies, and you shall be slaked. Bend one knee, and all knees shall bend to you. Wrath shall be yours and justice."

Rask called to him, but Zorsam did not hear. Manrix spoke and whether it was in his ear or in his soul, he did not know.

"Lift me up, my son, and I shall place you above all men, so that you may punish all who deserve it."

Hands grabbed his arm and pulled, but the strength was too little to move him. Zorsam stepped forward. Those black, blank eyes watched him. He knelt beside the fallen face, beside the terrible maw.

"My son," it whispered.

Zorsam reached out his hand to touch it.

With a sudden jolt of pain, he blacked out.

***

When he woke, Zorsam was in a small, dark room. Another moved as he stirred.

"You's awake!" Rask said. "Does yer head hurts?"

"Yes." He felt dried blood upon his scalp and a tremendous bump.

"Don't be mad. I had ta stops you somehow."

Zorsam sat up. The memories of what had happened were returning. "What did you do?"

"Threw piece o' dat idol dat broke off, I dids. Hard as I could." Rask stood several steps away, watching Zorsam cautiously. "Dat was Manrix, huh?"

Zorsam stood. "We must follow Margruxks."

"We don't know where he's going."

"He'll go to the Tower Xalthu soon. That is where the ceremony will be. We must move now." He took a step toward the door.

"Not dat way," Rask said, moving to block it. "Dat's where Manrix is."

"It is just an idol."

"Look at me," Rask said firmly. "I seen what happened. I didn't hears everying, but I seen enough. We goes 'nother way."

"Little Rat is scared of a statue."

"I's scared o' you."

"I will slay Margruxks. I will bring vengeance upon him. It is my right."

"Who's vengeance, Zorsam? Yers? Or de Great One's?"

"We are in agreement. His vengeance is mine, and mine is his. Have you forgotten that I was called by Death for this? I am a sword, and I shall slay. Do you want vengeance, little man? Or will you run away?"

"I's done running."

"Good." Zorsam found his sword against the wall and took it up. "We go to Xalthu to finish this. Come."

CHAPTER 11: The Gathering Storm

The Tower Xalthu spread its base broad and heavy across the valley, rising level by level toward the sky until it pierced the clouds with the sharp edges of its architecture. The black ziggurat cast its shadow over the thousands of slaves laboring beneath hard eyes and the bite of whips. Smoke rose from ceremonial fires along the base, the billows veiling and unveiling the grotesque images carved on the ever-ascending platforms. The lifeless sockets of a thousand idols gazed upon the sea of flesh below in pitiless contempt.

North of the Tower the skeleton of a forest remained. Xalthu had consumed it as it consumed everything in sight. Dead trees and hacked stumps were all that remained as Xalthu rose to the heavens. Margruxks would place his throne upon the pinnacle and rule over the Earth as a god.

Zorsam looked upon the Tower from the splintered forest. He saw the desolation and heard the moans and chains and clanging metal. And he smoldered.

Rask returned from his foraging and shared some wild berries and herbs with Zorsam. He ate them and, grunting, started toward the slave camp with Rask scrambling to keep up.

Darkness crept over the valley as Zorsam and Rask slinked into the camp. Old men stood in pits stomping mud and straw with tired legs. Young men hauled logs and blocks of stone. Women gathered grain and planted seeds in the fields. They worked with weary rhythm, their rags soaked with sweat in the thick evening heat. They glanced at Zorsam as he passed, marking his presence before returning to the work.

The Tower loomed above as they pressed in, deeper toward the inner turmoil of construction. Here, a foreman shouted, "Put your backs into it!" The crack of a whip punctuated the order.

They came to a giant wheel lying on its side. A dozen men pushed the grips along its edge in endless revolutions. Beneath the wheel was a deep pit which housed two massive grinding stones. Upon the center of the wheel stood a tall man in light Glaur armor. In his hand was a cat-o-nine-tails.

"Faster, you Dangray dogs!" he shouted.

The whip struck. A slave stumbled and collapsed, his back bloodied. The others struggled to keep the wheel turning, feet digging into the packed dirt.

"Rise, you worthless maggot!" demanded the soldier. "Now!"

The injured man was on all fours, trying to push himself to his feet. He stood and tried to retake his place. The wheel was slowing, the men exhausted; and though they leaned forward, groaning, it came to a stop.

"Turn the wheel!" the soldier spat, flicking the whip at the others. "It must turn! Get it started!" he screamed at the one who had first stumbled. "The wheel turns or you die."

The slave grabbed the rod and pushed, straining, legs taut and trembling. The others joined him, unsteady on their feet. Zorsam strode forward, sword drawn.

The soldier pulled back his whip. "Time's up, maggot."

The whip never snapped. Zorsam's sword entered the soldier's back and exited his chest. The man coughed blood and fell to his knees.

Zorsam leaned down to his ear as life left the skewered soldier. "Tell Death his acolyte sends his regards."

The barbarian wrenched his sword out. The soldier crumpled. Blood stained the wood of the wheel and dripped into the pit.

"He is the first," Zorsam told the slaves surrounding him. "Others will follow. You, also, are the first. Others will follow you into freedom."

"Who are you?" It was the slave who had stumbled that spoke.

Zorsam looked at him clearly for the first time. "Shamgar," he said, recognizing the slave from his vision.

The slave snorted. "And how do you know my name?"

Zorsam stepped down and stood in front of Shamgar. Though the slave had a warrior's body, Zorsam stood taller. "I saw you in a vision."

Shamgar laughed, but his face became thoughtful. "I suggest you stop drinking viperflower nectar. That poison won't help you work harder." He looked at the dead soldier. "Nor will it justify what you've done."

"If it brings Margruxks to me, so be it."

"You are mad. The king will flay your skin and let the birds eat your organs while you still live. And we will suffer as well."

"He alone will be punished."

"Who are you to claim such things?"

The voice that replied was a small one, but no less confident: "Dis is Zorsam de avenger, sent by de Great One himself."

Shamgar stepped back. "You are... Zorsam? You live?"

"I do."

Shamgar shook his head. "It's not possible. Asundi always believed…"

"She shall be rescued. I have come to mete out the Great One's wrath and to rescue my people."

Shamgar's eyes brightened. "Our God has not forsaken us. I must take you to Manoah, an elder of our tribe."

"I have heard of him as well in my visions. Let us make haste."

***

The slave camp was a hive of tents pressed one against another. Torch stands illuminated the faces of worn, empty people ready for a dreamless night's sleep where they might escape for a time.

Shamgar led Zorsam and Rask through the placid swarm. He had given them discarded cloaks to hide them from the guards' suspicion. Even here, away from the constant supervision of Glaur, they kept hoods up. Many would spread word in exchange for a moment of their oppressor's favor.

"This is Manoah's tent," said Shamgar as they arrived at one larger than the others. "I will go in first to—"

Zorsam pushed Shamgar aside and entered.

Two men, dressed in rags but with the presence of warriors, took combative postures as he entered. Zorsam touched the hilt of his sword.

"He's a friend," Shamgar said, following Zorsam. Rask slipped in as well.

Between the warriors was a wooden table. Sitting at the table was a grizzled old man with white hair and a beard peppered with black. He peered at Zorsam with gray eyes. His sinewy hands remained folded before him.

"You are Dangray," he said, "but you have been scarred by the wilderness, not by exile and the slave pits. Your face is one of defiance. Glaur has not yet conquered you. I do not think one such as yourself would ever bow. Speak. Who are you?"

"I am Zorsam. I am the hammer of the Great One."

Manoah's forehead crinkled. "Leave us," he told the warriors, who obeyed. He nodded thoughtfully. "Asundi spoke of you often."

"So I have seen in my visions."

"Visions?"

"Once, I lived as a beast. Then, after Death led me to himself, he taught me of men and of the Great One. After he had taught me, he gave me a mission. That is why I am here."

"What is this mission?"

"To crush Margruxks and slay all who do evil. Our people shall be avenged."

Manoah rested his forehead against his folded hands. He was silent and seemed to be praying. When he looked up, his eyes were shimmering. "The Great One has heard our cries. Is it possible?"

"I have come quickly, over many miles, striving to arrive before Margruxks. Do you know if Asundi has been brought? I will stop the ceremony and destroy the king."

Manoah looked to Shamgar. "This afternoon, I heard that she has been taken into the inner sanctum of the Tower. The king is preparing his body elsewhere, as demanded by his god, and he will perform the sacrifice when he arrives."

"When?" Zorsam demanded.

"I don't know. Soon."

"Then I will storm the Tower tonight."

"Not alone!" Shamgar said, grabbing Zorsam's arm. "I'm coming with you."

Zorsam pulled free. "Do not restrain me!"

"He is right, Zorsam," Manoah said. "You are strong, but even you cannot defeat the Glaur legion guarding the Tower. And even if you were able to infiltrate the Tower unseen, Asundi is guarded by two warriors with mystical powers."

"The Brothers," Zorsam spat.

"You know them. Shamgar here is a brave warrior and would assist you greatly. Unfortunately, he is one of only a few. Most of our warriors were killed in battle or executed to weaken us. What remains of the Dangray spirit is broken."

"It cannot be," Zorsam insisted. "Mine is not broken."

Manoah shook his head. "We are not all as strong as you. You were spared the long pursuit and continual defeat. You have been chosen by the Great One. But I don't believe you can reach the Tower alone, and I don't believe our people have the will to stand beside you."

Rask had remained silent in the shadows, but now he spoke. "I dinks once dey sees hope, dey haf will enough."

Zorsam looked at his friend. "Rask is right. Appearance does not matter. Nor does size. Vision is enough." He drew forth his sword and set it before him, hands upon the hilt, point upon the ground. "I will see my people now as I saw them in my vision. I will muster their strength, and we will swarm over the fields of battle to avenge the wrong done us. And I will have my vengeance."

"You speak like a king going to war." A weak smile cracked Manoah's face. It did not linger. "Is it your war or the Great One's?"

"They are one and the same."

"I hope you are right," the old man replied. "Men are cunning creatures, and we are able to deceive ourselves as easily as one another." He glanced at Rask. "And hope is as often a lie as not. Do you truly believe the legions can be turned back by men who have accepted slavery? Or do you mean to slay us for your vengeance?"

"Jackals can overtake larger prey, and insects can strip the skin from a carcass," said Zorsam. "A man may die alone, but a company may fight and live. That is what I think."

"You don't know," Shamgar said. "You've lived and fought alone, and now you want us to trust you. Even if we take the Ttwer, the entire army will assail us. We will be overrun. You'll slaughter us all."

"Then we will meet Death bravely and look him in the face without shame."

"Mebbe dat warn't be nessary."

Everyone looked at Rask.

"I kin go ta Garr and ask Prince Zarn fer help."

"Who?" Shamgar asked.

"Margruxks put him in charge o' an army. I knows. I's dere when it happened. We knows each other."

Zorsam nodded. "I have heard the story."

"Would this prince listen to you?" Manoah asked.

"Don't know," Rask said with a shrug. "But we don't haves any ot'er choice. Glaur's conquered most o' de free peoples 'round here. Wif Zarn's men, we can holds off Margruxks' army, maybe. But none o' dat matters if we kin't take de Tower. If he completes dat ritual, we's all dead."

"What is this ritual?" Manoah asked. "He has sacrificed our women before, but I sense this is different."

Zorsam answered. "Margruxks intends to sacrifice Asundi to Manrix for a portion of the demon's power."

Manoah seemed to contract, as if his form were folding in on itself. "There is no time. We must act fast. It may take Margruxks a few days to prepare himself, but no more than that. He will waste no time returning."

"I agree. Let us make the plan and be about it."

Soon, a tattered map of Xalthu and the surrounding area lay between them on the table. Shamgar sat on one side, but Zorsam remained on his feet. "How many ways are there through the walls?"

"One," Shamgar said, pointing. "It is heavily guarded. There are a few gaps elsewhere, though… here and here, for instance, since construction is not finished. They will be sealed soon. Unless we get behind those walls and fortify our position, we cannot win."

"Can you gather enough former warriors to infiltrate the Tower?" Manoah asked.

Shamgar tapped the map thoughtfully. "Yes. Yes, I think I can. Give me a few days."

"You have two," Zorsam said. "Even then, we risk Asundi's death. I will not lose her."

"What do you know of her?" Shamgar demanded. "You think you can return and claim her?"

"I have a right. She was revealed to me in Death's abode."

"I think you are lying."

"I do not lie."

"Enough!" said Manoah. "If you wish to die, do it at the hands of your enemies, not each other's."

"You warn't wins an argument wif Zorsam," Rask said, elbowing Shamgar.

Shamgar turned a steely face to Zorsam. "I will find men. Enough for two groups of ten to twenty. It will be done."

"Good." Zorsam nodded. "You will lead one and I the other."

"What of the Brothers?" asked Manoah.

Zorsam growled quietly. "I will deal with them myself."

"Very well," said Shamgar. "We will need slaves to distract the guards so we can sneak in. Perhaps they could start a riot or attack the walls."

"We have slings, and we can make some crude bows and spears," said Manoah. "Perhaps the blacksmiths can 'borrow' a few swords and shields for us."

Zorsam nodded in approval. "The Tower will be ours."

"We still have to deal with the rest of the army afterward," Shamgar said. "We might take the Tower, but we have no hope of surviving a larger force."

"Dat's where I come in!" Rask said. "Trust me. I gets you Garr's help."

"Rask is persistent," Zorsam said. "I have not been able to loose him from my boot yet." He gave Rask a hard stare and suddenly burst into deep laughter.

Rask's nervous face lit up. "I leaves at dawn," he said, inflating his chest. "I talks him into comin', one way o' 'nuther. Ain't a prince who ain't rather be his own master. Or man, fer dat matter. Not o' my people."

"Let it be done," Manoah said, standing weakly. "Go now and rest and may the Great One give us victory."

***

Dawn came soon enough. In the gray twinges of sunrise, the camp still slept the leaden sleep of the dying. Soon, soldiers would arrive to drive the slaves to their day's labors. Zorsam stood alone in the empty path between tents, alert while the multitude slept, as if he stood alone among the dead. Rask came to him and together they threaded their way to Manoah's tent, where Shamgar waited. He held an ugly brown horse.

"You can ride, I hope," Shamgar asked Rask.

"I kin holds on an' kick an' yell." With help, Rask clambered on and held himself admirably well upon the horse's bare back.

"I couldn't manage a saddle without drawing notice," Shamgar said.

65

Rask shrugged, clinging the horse's mane with just a hint of anxiety. "I gots a way wif animals. Doncha worry."

"Return soon, then, Rask," said Shamgar. "And bring friends."

Rask smiled. "I will!"

Shamgar nodded, glanced at Zorsam who waited silently, then walked away. Zorsam laid his hand upon Rask's leg. "Final victory depends upon you. Do not fail."

"You gots a ways o' makin' a man feel good, Zorsam, you do."

"This is what I was made for. This is the end of the hunt. I will not let my teeth be shattered when I have my jaws upon the beast's neck."

"Zorsam," Rask said, and his voice was serious. "From whats I understand, Death showed you what it meant ta be a man an' not a beast. I saw what happened at Zorah -- remember, a beast reacts. What he does ain't right. It ain't wrong. It just is. But a man ain't a beast. A man kin do de right ding wrongly."

Zorsam's expression remained steely. "I have heard you, little man."

Rask sighed. "I warn't a spiritual man before, but I's praying ta de Great One fer you."

"Very well."

"Goodbye, Zorsam."

Rask nudged the horse. It stubbornly edged forward. He then slammed his heels in harder, and the horse galloped off, Rask nearly flying from it. It weaved through the curving, narrow pathway until it passed out of sight, Rask hanging on for dear life.

CHAPTER 12: Liberator

Six Glaur soldiers guarded the opening in the north wall of Tower Xalthu. It provided a convenient route for supplies into the incomplete structure and would be sealed as soon as it was no longer used. The guards looked out into the early morning twilight for movement, for signs of an attack. None had ever come.

A hundred feet from their station, two grinding wheels waited for their workers, who would soon arrive. In the pits beneath, dark forms crouched.

Zorsam, with nearly twenty warriors covered in dark war paint, waited. They had crept forth in the lengthening shadows and slid into the two pits to await the time of their attack. Dust and ground flour tickled Zorsam's nose. He peeked over the edge of the pit. One man was looking intently in their direction, as if he had heard the shifting of their feet. Zorsam watched from the deep darkness. Eventually the guard exchanged a word with the others and directed his attention elsewhere.

"I hope Shamgar and his men are in position," whispered the warrior next to Zorsam.

"Are you afraid?" the barbarian queried.

The young man nodded.

"Remember this fear. It is what our enemies will soon feel."

"Do you not fear?"

"I find it best not to ask the question."

It was not an answer. Within these walls waited two men who had twice defeated him. Once they were routed, he would still have to deal with Margruxks and his army. There was no word from Rask. To fear was to have something to lose; he did fear, deep within, but he was not certain what he feared. He did not think it was death. Perhaps it was failure -- to be the hammer that cracked instead of shattering the foe. He did not fear what might happen to the Great One's name if he failed.

Dawn crept along the land, unveiling the squalid camp. They heard the west gates open and the thunder of a legion marching out to drive the slaves to their work.

The signal would come soon.

They waited in the dimming darkness of the pits, aware of the noises of a city waking, the rising hum of life. Then came the tumult, a spike of voices and shouting. The soldiers at the wall turned their eyes west. Four retreated into the opening and ran toward the west gate.

Zorsam raised his hand and motioned the warriors forward.

Out of the two pits the war paint-smeared men rose, rushing along the fading shadows. Zorsam strode ahead, sword out. Beyond, the tumult gained an edge of violence. Battle had begun and there was no fear now, only the expectation before the clash.

The soldiers did not see them until it was too late. They were distracted by the sounds of conflict and did not see the sword approach. Zorsam ran his blade through one; another warrior slit the second's throat.

They slipped through the opening, running quick and quiet. Dangray battle cries rose in the air from the west. Glaur soldiers shouted orders. Iron clashed on iron. Arrows hissed through the air.

Vengeance was not his alone. It was the Dangray's. It was a people seeking justice.

Zorsam led them to the conflict. Glaur soldiers crowded the gate. Archers and black iron pots lined the parapets above. Smoke billowed from the pots as archers stabbed the hot coals within and fired them at the attacking slaves. Howls of pain rose from the swarming slaves as fire and sword fell upon them.

By sheer numbers, they were overwhelming the Glaur soldiers, but they fell in dozens beneath the blows. Zorsam saw the slaughter and he remembered the fields of death that had greeted him upon his emergence into the world of men. A desire to protect his people, the understanding of vengeance as the sharp edge of mercy, overwhelmed him.

"Attack!" he roared, and he charged, leading his men up the steps to the parapet.

While the Dangray focused the soldiers' attention, Zorsam and his men could do their work. They cut through the archers, disrupting their assault, and, seeing that others could handle the rest, he leapt down into the fray below, working with his sword as an explorer with his machete to clear a path for others. The soldiers turned on him, but he knew why he fought and he knew how to destroy. Their shields shattered beneath his sword. Their armor cracked like eggshells.

In time, his companions rejoined him, and together they began to push the enemy back, out the gate. Zorsam stepped away from the conflict for a moment to gain his bearings. The sun had risen. He could see the gaping entry of Tower Xalthu. Within, Asundi waited to be sacrificed.

Shamgar appeared at his side. "Go," he said.

"She is only one. I have men to kill here."

Shamgar grabbed Zorsam's shoulder. "Fool! She waited for a deliverer for years. Will you squander your call in slaughter when you could save?"

Zorsam nodded. Shamgar spoke rightly, though it was logic strange to him. The blood of Margruxks and his men should be on his hands -- that was vengeance. But the Brothers would be guarding Asundi, and he desired a rematch.

"You must clear the gates and let the slaves in," said Zorsam. "Only then will the Tower be ours."

"It will be done. Go!"

Zorsam closed the distance to the doors with long strides. He slashed those who tried to slow him, leaving blood and death in his wake. He leapt up the stairs to the door.

He smelled the brimstone a moment before flames erupted from the opening. The force of the heat threw him to his back. When he looked again, the Brothers swaggered into the morning light, flames dancing in Zaduk's hands, a scimitar of ice shimmering in Fria's.

"You never do learn, do you?" said Zaduk.

This was why he had come. Not for Asundi. Not for victory. For a taste of the Brothers' blood. For the feel of their bones breaking.

He lunged forward, growling. He dodged Zaduk's fireball and struck. At the last moment, Zaduk parried with his own sword and sparks flew.

"Welcome back, barbarian." The fire-warrior forced a smile, then ignited his sword. The sudden blast forced Zorsam to step back.

When he looked past the wave of heat, he saw that Fria had erected a wall of ice, blocking his passage into the Tower.

"None shall pass," said Fria.

The Brothers struck. Zorsam parried Zaduk's burning blade, sidestepping Fria's slice. Zaduk pressed hard, attacking again and again. Zorsam blocked blow after blow, moving in circles to keep Fria at a distance. Pressed near the wall, Zorsam knocked Zaduk's sword against the stones and held it there with his blade as his free hand struck the fire-warrior so hard in the face that his head smacked into the wall. Zorsam followed with a kick that knocked Zaduk's grip loose and sent his sword clattering to the ground.

A flash of fire drove Zorsam back into a cold blade. Fria's sword slashed his back and Zorsam spun, gritting against the pain. He managed to deflect Fria's next strike, though his arm went numb as frost traveled from Fria's blade into Zorsam's own sword and froze his hands stiff.

Another slash ignited his back, an X of blood now carved there. He used the sudden pain to launch himself forward. He elbowed Fria with the entire force of his body and pressed past, twirling and coming to a defensive stance before Zaduk could close the gap.

Men were climbing the stairs toward them, shouting battle cries. The Dangray had taken the gates and he saw several of his warriors leading the assault upon the Brothers.

Zaduk saw them too. He inhaled, blew flames into his hands, and then scattered them. They fell like rain upon the steps and rose up in pillars of fire, barring the way.

"Your friends weren't invited," Zaduk said. "This dance is between the three of us." He sighed deeply. "Now, *burn!*"

Fire gushed from his mouth. Zorsam charged into it, rolling beneath the liquefied air. As he stood, ice-darts pierced his shoulders and thighs. He staggered as his limbs numbed, but he pressed forward, swinging his sword at Zaduk, who parried. Fria attacked, but Zorsam managed to deflect his scimitar, and Zaduk pushed his brother out of the way to hammer Zorsam with his own sword. Their blades met with a shock of metal.

Locked together, they pressed against one another. Zorsam strained his muscles, edging Zaduk's blade back. He roared, forcing his muscles to move. He met Zaduk's eyes, saw the red glare there, and pressed. Flames licked at

Zorsam's face, and his palms burned on the hilt of his sword. Zaduk held his advance and began, slowly, imperceptibly, to push Zorsam back.

"Give my regards to the Underworld!" Zaduk said.

Suddenly, his eyes flashed and the flames on his sword flared. Zorsam staggered back, nearly blinded. The death blow was coming. Instinct kicked in. Faster than conscious thought, Zorsam dropped his sword, intercepted his adversary's arm, and with a bestial roar, threw Zaduk over his shoulder and slammed him to the ground.

His vision was just returning, and he blinked the searing tears from his eyes. He lurched forward. The sharp bite of ice-darts dug into his back. In the corner of his hazy vision he saw his sword, still glowing red.

He dove for it, seizing the searing hilt and standing, already moving forward to meet Fria.

Their blades clashed. Zorsam's hot sword cut through Fria's scimitar and continued forward, slashing Fria across the chest. He kept the momentum, spinning, and thrust the sword into the ice-warrior. The man gagged and fell to his knees. His blood sizzled on the sword's blade. He expelled clouds of fog and collapsed.

"No!"

Zorsam stooped down as he turned to face Zaduk. He grabbed the point of Fria's ice-scimitar from the ground and, with a flick, launched it through the air. It struck the fire-warrior in the forehead. Zaduk wailed, clutching the wound as hot blood and steam gushed forth. He fell and screamed and flailed as the ice-blade boiled and scalded his face. Slowly, he became still.

Zorsam straightened himself. He breathed deeply and let himself feel the pain of his injuries. He lived. His foes were dead.

He could not release the sword. His skin had melted to the hilt.

Below soldiers still stood upon the steps. The flames had not died out with Zaduk's death. The wall of ice blocking entry into the temple still waited. Zorsam stood alone, bloody, victorious.

Asundi.

He did not know if one of those below had shouted her name or if some part of his conscience had spoken. In the beginning, he had been captivated by her. Now, her memory stirred no emotion, except a desire to slay Margruxks. He had lost something; he had been sharpened to a point that allowed no distraction. He pierced others and, somehow, could not be pierced.

He strode to the wall of ice. She lay within. Could he truly be *man* without another? He had gained some dimension from Rask he had not known with Death. What might Asundi reveal to him? Did he care?

He had once felt some such emotion.

He struck the wall with his blade. A crack split the ice, but the wall did not shatter. Zorsam struck again. The crack expanded. He pounded it with the hilt, his arm growing stronger, his will adding its resolve. Shards peppered his body and cooled his warm flesh.

With one last blow the wall shattered and, with a shove, fell to the floor in pieces.

He walked through the dark hallway. Dim torchlight lit a room ahead. The ceiling rose as he approached until he stood at the edge of a large, dark sanctuary. It smelled of smoke and blood. Grotesque statues sat upon the wall, their tortured faces turned toward the altar, over which the great wolf Manrix waited, snarling. The black marble of his face shimmered with reflected firelight.

Beneath his jaws, upon the altar, lay Asundi.

He would not enter this place armed. This woman who had been his first glimpse of hope would not wake to a man ready to attack. He forced his hand open. His skin tore as he severed hand from hilt. The sword fell to the ground with a dull clang, and he howled in pain.

He approached warily, with a sense of fear and uncertainty he had not felt in a long time. He did not know now what she was or what he was. She was not prize or foe but another, unlike him and yet like, a friend in times since forgotten by his harsh life, a mysterious entity of which others spoke with reverence. He, a man of sword and blood and violence, approached one pure and undefiled.

He stopped before the altar. For the third time, he saw her in the flesh with his own eyes. White silk garments covered her chest and waist. White skirt extended to her knees. Her arms lay strong and motionless at her sides. Her bronze legs carried the strength of many miles. A crimson tiara was in her black hair.

He reached to touch her smooth face. It was marred as a placid lake beneath which the shark swims. It was a shimmer of pain upon a pure visage. His fingers brushed her skin --

and a shock of energy knocked him back. He grunted, cradling his bloody hand.

"She is mine, beast."

He knew the voice. The black orbs of the idol glinted with fire.

"Do you desire her?" the voice continued. "Do you wish to feel her skin against your own? She is mine, and I am able to grant you your desire."

"I am Death's messenger," Zorsam said. "I do not fear you."

"I am intimate with Death. Neither do I fear you."

"I am the Great One's wrath."

"You kill. What have you to do with this woman? Slay her if you wish to free her from my grip. It will be a mercy, no? She is in a death-sleep, waiting to complete the ceremony that will separate soul from body and allow me to consume her fully. Do you wish to save her? Pierce her with your sword. That is what you are meant for -- death and blood and vengeance."

Zorsam tore his eyes from Manrix and attempted to grab Asundi's arm, to break her free. Energy coursed through his body. He roared, trying to press his hand forward, but he could not. His strength, his will, could not bear the force that pressed against him, that sizzled beneath the skin and squeezed his head. He stepped back, his body trembling.

"Where is the Great One? Did he not give you power to match mine? You are no sword. You are a broken arrow. He will launch another soon, and one after that, hoping someday to slay me. You will be trampled long before that. Your people will die. Death will usher you into dark places from which you will never return."

Outside, faint shouts of victory rose, and Zorsam heard them as if from another world. The Dangray had taken the Tower. They had succeeded. Now they would wait for Margruxks to come against them with his army.

"Join them," Manrix said. "Let them praise you for slaying the Brothers. Let them bury their dead and sing songs to you. When my son arrives, he shall crush you, and this woman shall be devoured.

"If you wish to destroy, beast, if you wish to drink the blood of your enemies and take this woman as your own, come to me. Vengeance is mine and always shall be."

"No! I am the sword and I am the destroyer!"

Manrix did not answer. His idol stood dark and heavy and silent. Finally, Zorsam turned away. At the entrance to the sanctuary, he took hold of his sword once more. Through the black hallway he walked until he emerged into the light.

Men celebrated in the courtyard below, and when they saw him, they began to chant, "Hail Zorsam! Hail Zorsam the Liberator!"

CHAPTER 13: The Silent God

Dusk settled on Xalthu, the steps of the incomplete ziggurat falling to darkness one by one. Zorsam walked in its shadow, along the walls his men had entered four days previous. Even in the dim light he could see the patches that completed the wall, the mortar weak because they made it quickly. One well-placed shot from Glaur's catapults would shatter the repairs.

He climbed the steps to the top of the wall and looked out at the fields in one direction and the slave camps in the other. Much of the fighting had happened near the Tower, followed by skirmishes throughout the camps for two days. They put out the fires that remained. Now only a scattering of torches lit the darkening land. Shamgar's men moved in that light, making final adjustments to the traps. The women and children hid in the basement storerooms of the Tower, the safest location they could manage. It may be a temple to a demon, but its foundation was firm and the storerooms constructed as defensible as a fortress. The men patrolled the camp and prepared for battle.

A runner arrived an hour ago with news. Margruxks would arrive at dawn.

Rask had not returned, and he still sent no word. The might of Margruxks would smash against Xalthu in the morning. Zorsam's men were brave, and some were fighters, but they would not survive the day.

Tomorrow, Zorsam would fight and he would slay, and he would die upon the field of battle. He would seek out Margruxks, if he could, but he would not return alive from the encounter.

Zorsam remained looking over the land until the sun was extinguished, and the world was wrapped in night. The stars shone bright above.

Zorsam knelt upon the cold stone. He had worshipped the Great One in the beginning and he had spoken of him throughout his journey. Now he dared to speak to him directly.

"Is this the purpose you called me to? Am I to be shattered for you?"

The Great One did not answer. Manrix spoke to him, but the Great One did not. He had sent Death to teach him instead. Was he too bloody to hear his voice? Did the Great One speak, yet he heard naught but wind?

The barbarian stood again and returned to the courtyard. Tomorrow, Dangray warriors would assemble here to defend their families and their freedom. Their vengeance upon Margruxks was to live and defend that life.

Stopping in the middle of the courtyard, Zorsam looked up at the Tower Xalthu. Its point impaled the moon.

"Zorsam!"

Zorsam waited for the voice to continue. It was the demon-wolf. This was still his domain.

"Will you really die here? Will you watch your people die? I will devour their souls when they come to me."

Zorsam said nothing. The spire that impaled the moon seemed to change the white orb into immense jaws, ready to engulf the world.

"You kneel before the Silent God. Kneel before me. I will grant you power and strength and glory and honor. What Margruxks has, you shall take, and whatever you desire shall be yours."

The words fell heavily upon him, like a mantle of iron. He wanted to stagger beneath the weight of them. He wanted to fall to his knees and take what was offered, and yet—

He raised his head until he saw only stars and he roared. "Where are you, Great One? Show yourself! Answer this demon! Where is the favor you showed me? Where is it?"

The gate behind him opened. He turned, wary, and saw a cloaked man enter upon a horse. The horse trotted up to him.

"I did not hear the words, but I heard the sound," said Manoah. "Do you wish to scare Margruxks or us?"

Zorsam met Manoah's gaze with a scowl.

The old man dismounted. "I came to speak with you."

"Then speak."

"You are much as I imagine your teacher was. Single-minded, brutal, serious."

"That is what I am. He was not."

"When we are finished here. What will you be? Will you still thirst for blood?"

"We will not leave here. This is our grave. Then you will meet my teacher."

"No. If I am to die, I will then meet the Great One. Seeing a person's shadow is not the same as seeing him, Zorsam. I think you have mistaken the servant for the master and the weapon for the blacksmith."

"I am the weapon."

"A storm is a weapon in his hand. An earthquake is his weapon. You are a man. You may be his hammer for a time, but you are not merely a hammer. You have a choice. I do not know what the Great One has revealed to you or what his plans are for you, but with your arrival I have learned once again to trust in his wisdom. But I did not come to say these things to you. I came to give you a gift."

He opened the saddlebag and produced a strange shape of fur. As Manoah straightened it, Zorsam saw it for what it was, a headdress designed like a mane.

"Our people consider the lion a symbol of the Great One's strength and nobility. When a man wishes to become chieftain, he journeys into the wilderness to face a lion. If he slays it, he wears its skin and mane as a sign that the Great One has chosen him. It also reminds him that he is to be a servant of the Great One, wearing his skin, so to speak."

Manoah offered Zorsam the headdress.

"We have no chieftain. You have been chosen by the Great One. Wear this tomorrow as you lead our men. May it remind you of your call and of your responsibilities."

Zorsam took the mane. "I bring only death."

"If we die tomorrow or if we live, that is not your doing. You are responsible for following the call you have been given. Lead our people and serve the Great One. Do you understand?"

"I do not know."

"In the morning, we will find out if you do." Manoah mounted his horse. "Until then, I shall pray for you and our people. Good night, Zorsam."

Zorsam watched the old man go. He set the headdress upon himself. Was he man or beast?

He did not know. He was not sure he cared. He was a weapon. That he knew. That he could understand. And that he could be.

CHAPTER 14: The Black Tide

Zorsam stood upon the wall before dawn, dressed for battle in leather armor taken from one of the slain Glaur soldiers. The lion's mane hung around him, and he gripped his sword, freshly sharpened, in his strong hand. A beast with teeth to tear and rip.

The Tower's shadow slithered forward as the sun rose. Beyond it, a sea of men advanced like a black tide. They bore crimson banners with the black wolf upon it. Forward they marched in a steady rhythm, relentless. The morning light shone on their armor and on the hundreds of chariots pulled by black warhorses. The catapults groaned forward between them.

The Dangray stood ready for battle, but as they looked out upon the horde, they whispered to one another. They were too few. They wore ragtag armor, wielded second-hand weapons. An archer began to raise his bow, but Shamgar commanded him to lower it.

Rask had not returned. It was too late now. Here, Zorsam would pile the dead before him as long as he had breath. If Death wanted him to avenge his people and mete out justice, he would do it until the end.

The Glaur army stopped at the edge of the valley. The infantry parted, and a chariot pulled by a pair of three-horned beasts drove forward. It was blood-red, highlighted by glinting gold. The driver was a man wearing a skull mask and a black cape.

Margruxks. Zorsam felt the dark anticipation in his muscles. The time had come for judgment.

Margruxks raised his hand high and motioned. His army advanced in lines, trampling the slaves' golden grain. Behind the infantry, men loaded the catapults with stones.

"Archers, ready!" shouted Shamgar.

Every warrior lining the battlements touched his arrow to a nearby bowl of hot coals, prepared for the purpose, then raised his bow and pulled back as the arrows sparked into flame.

"Fire!"

The arrows arched through the sky, but they did not land among the soldiers. The flaming tips fell into the fields on either side. With a roar and a flash, fire erupted in the prepared crops and quickly spread, rushing toward the soldiers and catapults. The flames reached the flanks before the soldiers could retreat, and the first lines broke in confusion. The stench of burning flesh and oil rose up in dark billows of smoke.

The Dangray roared in triumph, but Zorsam kept his eyes upon Margruxks.

The army quickly reformed, finding paths around and through the flaming fields. It would burn a long time, according to the men who had prepared the land for this moment. But soon, cavalry and foot soldiers were again assembled and charging forward.

The ground beneath the Glaur legion collapsed. Men and beast tumbled into holes, shrieking as they were impaled on makeshift spears. The land before the Tower was pocked with pits into which beast and man fell and never returned.

The front line slowed.

"Fire!" cried Zorsam.

Arrows sprang forth and pierced the hesitant soldiers below. A second wave followed, slamming into the army before the Tower. By now, some of the soldiers managed to hold up shields, but they did not advance.

Margruxks's chariot raced along the front of the army, and his voice rose above the din of fire and dying men. "Advance! Do not stop. Those who hesitate will meet my sword. Take the Tower!"

"Come to me," Zorsam said softly. "Not your men. You."

The men began to run forward, gathered again into small companies, shields lifted high. Behind, the catapults had been anchored into position, the fires that threatened them contained.

At Shamgar's command, wave after wave of arrows fell upon the enemy, but bows had been in short supply. Others wielded slings, and now they unleashed their rocks upon the incoming army. Warriors waited with sword and spear for the close combat to begin.

The catapults snapped forward, launching boulders toward them.

"Get down!" Zorsam commanded. His men obeyed, but he remained standing and watched the boulders descend.

They soared over his head, one so close he might have touched it with his sword, and crashed into the courtyard. Men screamed. Zorsam absorbed their suffering and waited for Margruxks to approach. He would avenge their deaths.

The army pressed against the walls like a black sea. Siege ladders appeared, and men unloaded a tremendous battering ram with the visage of Manrix upon it. Margruxks stood in his chariot and watched the assault through his skull mask.

Zorsam raised his sword. It gleamed in the new day. His voice thundered across the walls and over the fields. "For vengeance!"

Below, men loaded crossbows. Arrows hissed through the air and struck men to Zorsam's right and left. They stumbled back with the force of impact, and one fell off the parapet to the ground below. Another round of boulders rained down. Many hit the wall, shards of rock breaking off and slashing the arms and faces of the defenders, but some landed in the courtyard and scattered the men assembled there.

Foot soldiers set their ladders against the wall in the confusion and climbed.

"They're coming!" Zorsam cried, motioning for more warriors to join him.

The first of the soldiers were nearly at the top. With a great heave, Zorsam pushed the closest ladder back. It teetered for a moment before falling into the sea of men below.

Others had already topped the wall. Growling, Zorsam cut through them with his sword, pushing them aside and to their death. Shamgar, whirling his bladed stave, patrolled the other direction. Dangray men armed with swords and spears bounded up the stairs and entered the fray. Archers stabbed the enemy with arrows, gouging eyes when they could. Blood spread across the parapets. Limbs, heads, and bodies rained from the wall. But for each soldier slain and ladder pushed back, more took their place.

Catapults snapped. Boulders smashed against the walls. The north wall broke open. As Zorsam looked, the Glaur army poured through like blood from a wound.

"Defend the breach!"

Dangray warriors rushed to it. The battle raged tight and fierce. The Glaur pressed forward by sheer mass, but the Dangray were caged and wild, attacking with a ferocity that mirrored Zorsam's own. Bodies fell in heaps at the breach, slowing the enemy, and the Dangray stood their ground, unyielding, as their fellows engaged those who had entered. Finally, Zorsam's men pressed forward over the bodies of companions and enemies and bottlenecked the Glaur at the breach.

Booming thuds echoed through the air. While Zorsam's men stopped the gap, the enemy had begun to ram the main gate.

"Shamgar! The gate!" he yelled.

Shamgar commanded his slingers to direct their attacks at those holding the ram. Taking up broken pieces of wall, the slingers let them fly. They struck their targets, but men replaced those who had fallen. A slinger gurgled and fell as an arrow pierced his throat. There was no one to replace him.

The crack of the door split the air. The hideous wolf head slammed through the gate.

The noises of war dimmed around Zorsam. He looked to the implacable face of Margruxks, who sensed his stare and raised his eyes to the barbarian. He stood regal and terrible in his crimson chariot, his army surrounding him, and the great three-horned beasts snorting in impatience beneath the firm grip of his reins.

Zorsam had known the wall would fail. Some part of him had waited for it to fail. It made his mission clearer, his responsibility narrower. Now, he could descend into the fray and meet Margruxks one-on-one. This sea of humanity did not matter. He would kill Margruxks; his blood would soak into the ground; his body would grow cold, and the birds would eat his flesh. That is what Zorsam wanted to see and feel before he died. Surely, Death gave him humanity that he might bring death to those who deserved it.

Zorsam bared his teeth, bellowed a roar, and jumped to the ground. Glaur soldiers looked up. One turned fast enough to see his death coming. Zorsam's sword cleaved his helmet and split his skull. Dislodging the weapon, he turned and decapitated the next soldier. For a moment, the other soldiers hesitated. Zorsam rushed them. One by one, he cut them down. They slashed him, but he barely noticed. Pain simply reminded him he still had breath to destroy.

Above the din, Zorsam heard stone sundering. He broke away from the fight for a moment to find its source. Nearby, black-clad soldiers swarmed through a new hole in the wall. His men were barely holding the north wall as it was. If he could not reach the battlefield, if he was unable to face Margruxks man-to-man—

A horn sounded.

It came again, a bright, golden note. A strange light feeling entered his angry, blood-soaked mind and he raised his head. He waited for the note again. It came, and he found himself among a dozen dead bodies, surrounded by injured, moaning men. The sound was like the pinprick of the light of the world above as one ascends from Death's chamber.

He ignored the men moving toward him. He found the nearest steps and climbed them. He turned, hand shading his eyes, and to the south he saw it. Bright yellow banners, and beneath them marched orderly columns of men. Before them, upon a white horse, was a little man wearing purple, and beside him an even smaller man. Zorsam knew him, though he was too far away to see his face clearly.

"The men of Garr!" he shouted. "They have arrived! Rask is here!"

Zorsam remained for a moment, looking at the reinforcements. He wanted to wait for them, to hold back from the death below, but the battle was hot and fierce. He descended into the mass of men, giving himself over to his instincts once more. He fought and killed, and yet there was a lightness to his movements. This was not the final stand. Men might still live. He might still live. He had been ready to join Death, but he found that now, having heard the trumpet and seen Rask, he did not *want* to.

Soon, hundreds of short men in polished armor moved in among the Dangray. They fought with the tenacity of rodents, carving a dozen paths through the Glaur ranks to the holes in the wall. Zorsam worked with sword to widen the area so they could help hold the breach.

He sensed a Glaur soldier behind him, one who had been severed from his army. Zorsam turned to defend himself, but a small man jumped onto the soldier's back, stabbing him in the neck with his daggers. The soldier fell, and the small man raised his head from the enemy, smiling.

"Do I hafs ta do everyding?"

"Rask!"

"De one an' only!"

"I did not know you could fight."

"You never asked."

Zorsam grinned, a strange feeling of brotherhood dawning.

"Where's Asundi?"

"In the temple. I must kill Margruxks first."

Rask eyed Zorsam, searching his face. "I's been dinkin'. It ain't *just* fer men ta die who ain't deserve it."

"He deserves death!" Zorsam roared.

Rask stepped back but did not cower. "I don't means him. Ev'ryone else. Who's fightin' fer dem? I is. My people is. Just -- remember. You ain't never been among men, but dat's de reason fer being human, ta be among dem."

Beyond the wall an agonized roar rose above the battle. Zorsam looked to the smoldering fields. Margruxks whipped his strange beasts to charge, crushing the men before him and causing his chariot to career precariously around the many pits. Before him, a squadron of his personal guard ran, dispatching those in his way.

Zorsam saw nothing but Margruxks as he left Rask and charged forward, sword cutting a path through bodies. He passed through the broken gate, out onto the battlefield. There he stood, as if he alone would bar the way, and Margruxks saw him and drove his chariot forward. Friend and foe alike moved to escape the headlong path of the chariot, but Zorsam stood, unmoved, feet spread, sword sheathed, arms outstretched. The horned beasts barreled forward, towering over him, and when he could smell the stink of their breath, he leaped, grasping the horns of one. It shook wildly but he held fast, roaring, his eyes on his nemesis.

Margruxks lashed his whip at Zorsam. It tore into Zorsam's flesh, but he pulled in the pain, compressed it, and let it strengthen him. His grip tightened and he pulled himself up, ready to pounce into the chariot.

The beasts smashed into the line of Garr and Dangray soldiers holding the gate. He heard their screams, and his attention was drawn from the skull mask to the men who bled and died around him. The whip slashed his arm. His grip loosened. He fell from his position and hit the ground.

He stood, surrounded by wounded men. He was within the walls near the courtyard. Garr and Dangray and Glaur fought in tight pockets. Margruxks was upon the steps of the Tower, racing up to the entrance.

Asundi was within, helpless. The leader of his people, the vision of his re-birth, his friend from times forgotten. With her Margruxks would seize the power of Manrix.

Zorsam did not consider that. In that brief, startling instant, he knew only that Asundi was *his*, and if he could protect no one else, he would protect her. She would suffer no harm, even if it required his blood soak the floors of the temple.

With speed beyond that of ordinary man, he pursued Margruxks.

CHAPTER 15: The Dark Struggle

The din of war echoed in the empty vestibule. It was dark, with only a few torches still burning. It mattered not. Zorsam stormed through the hallway to the inner sanctum, sure of his way through darkness and smoke.

He passed through the archway and saw Margruxks' black figure approach the altar. Asundi slept there defenseless beneath the gleaming eye of Manrix. A metal clatter echoed through the silent room as Margruxks discarded his mask. In his hand he held a dagger.

"No time for a priest," he said, looking up at the red eyes of the wolf-god. "No intermediary. I am prepared. I vouch for myself."

Then he spoke in a strange, vile tongue. He raised his dagger as he growled and bared his teeth. His words licked the shadowed walls of the sanctuary with a hungry, gnawing impatience.

Zorsam moved silently, hidden by these hateful words, and now he ran the last few paces, sword pulled back to strike.

The sword thrust forward, but Margruxks stepped aside and spun. His dagger sank deep into Zorsam's shoulder. The force of the blow and the pain knocked Zorsam to his knees.

Margruxks yanked the dagger out of the flesh and sinew. "Die!" he snarled, the accent of the dark tongue still in his voice.

Margruxks drew his sword with his other hand and struck. Zorsam parried weakly, pain shooting through his arm. Holding his hilt in both hands, he used it to push Margruxks away.

"Devour this soul," Margruxks said. "I will bring it to you, Manrix."

86

He lunged at Zorsam, striking in a rapid succession of blows. In the darkness Zorsam sensed the movements rather than saw them. Sparks flew from the swords as they clashed and sang; in silence Zorsam accepted wounds on arm and leg. Margruxks was faster and stronger and uninjured.

As another slash cut across his thigh, Zorsam hammered his free hand into the king's face. Margruxks flinched. Red shimmered upon his lip in the glowering light. Zorsam followed with a thrust, but Margruxks jumped back and took a defensive stance.

For the first time, Zorsam had a moment of rest.

Margruxks began to circle the barbarian, striking inward suddenly. He seemed to slide across the ground. Another wound opened upon Zorsam's side. Margruxks pulled back and circled again, waiting, watching, and suddenly struck.

This time Zorsam parried the sword, but Margruxks smashed his dagger into his shoulder wound and left it there. Zorsam caught the scream of pain in his teeth. Margruxks struck again with his sword. Zorsam, his arm weak, dropped his weapon and stopped the king's blade by catching the hilt in both hands, pressing the blade back toward Margruxks. The king kicked Zorsam and pulled away.

As Zorsam ripped the dagger from his shoulder, Margruxks lunged at him. A flurry of slashes, barely dodged, forced Zorsam back to the wall. He bumped into a brass torch pole, knocking it over and spilling acrid ashes. The sword glinted in the sudden flare of light. Zorsam ducked, and the king's sword lodged into the wall, spraying flecks of brick.

Zorsam turned to strike with his dagger, but Margruxks snatched a handful of soot and threw it into Zorsam's face. Zorsam turned away blinded, eyes burning. He staggered, knowing that the moment it took Margruxks to dislodge his sword saved him. He blinked and scrubbed and looked up.

Margruxks stood before him holding his own sword and Zorsam's.

He charged, and Zorsam backpedaled. His back hit another wall, crimson light flaring up at the king's approach. Zorsam grabbed the torch near him and swung it, burning Margruxks' face and sending one of the swords spinning across the floor. Zorsam dove for the weapon.

He stood before the altar, skin slick with blood, breathing heavily.

Behind him, Asundi moaned.

Zorsam glanced over his shoulder. His people's princess -- *his* princess -- was moving, jerking, as one unable to sleep.

Margruxks charged Zorsam. Zorsam blocked his swing and thrust his other hand out, striking Margruxks in the throat.

"No more!" Zorsam shouted. He hammered at the king with his sword, the clash of metal ringing forth and echoing. "We end this. You die now!"

Pain soaked Zorsam's muscles. He burned. Margruxks had driven him back for the last time. He was the slayer of evil men; here, now, he would end the life of the one who had caused so much misery; here, now, he would triumph over his foe and cut off his head and carry it into battle to show men and gods that Zorsam wrought justice with his hand and his sword. Here. Now.

Zorsam moved with a rage and bestial instinct. Margruxks held his own, backing away, but he suffered slash and cut. Zorsam held nothing back. He did not consider his safety or his life; he considered nothing at all except the living creature before him.

With a powerful blow, Zorsam severed Margruxks' hand. The sword and hand fell to the floor, and the king bellowed rage and hatred in his vile tongue.

"Kill him."

The voice came from the altar. Asundi sat upon it, hands upon her lap, black hair framing a shadowed face.

Zorsam grinned. She spoke the words that burned within him. He lunged forward. Margruxks had turned to Asundi in surprise. Now Zorsam saw his eyes turn to him. Zorsam saw the king's muscles tense. But the sword entered his gut. It rammed through him and out the back. Margruxks fell to his knees.

"It isn't—" His eyes widened and stared. "No," he muttered.

Zorsam pulled back his arm, and Margruxks fell to the floor. He moaned and breathed, but he would not live long.

Then Zorsam turned to Asundi, his sword wet with blood, his skin wet with blood, his mind filled with blood.

"Bring him to me," Asundi said. "I would look upon him."

Zorsam bent down and lifted his foe's body. It was heavy in his arms. His legs were weak now that the fight was over, but he forced them to move. Step by step he drew close to the princess. Her eyes blazed in the red light of the torches, and her lips shone like fire.

Zorsam stopped before her, and she reached a smooth hand to touch the wound in Margruxks' abdomen. Her fingers came away sticky with blood, which she rubbed between thumb and forefinger thoughtfully. She looked up at him.

"Zorsam." She smiled. "You have begun to show your wrath. This is the first." Asundi stepped off the altar, motioning to it. "Finish him."

Zorsam understood. He placed Margruxks upon the altar. His chest hardly moved, but he lived. Zorsam raised his sword and slammed it down. The altar shook and the whole room seemed to vibrate. Margruxks' head rolled away from his body.

Asundi's warm hand touched his wounded shoulder. He turned toward her, and she leaned close, until he could feel her breath upon his face.

"Kiss me," she said. "Take me."

In that moment, in that silent instance, Zorsam could hear his heart and he could hear hers. Beneath it, somewhere, were the shouts and cries of men dying outside the temple. He heard men shouting to their gods, to Manrix, to the Great One -- to him, Zorsam.

Asundi leaned in, her nose brushing his own. A deep desire rose in him, a desire to have her and own her and conquer her. His hands pulled her close. She did not resist. His lips were upon hers, and he held her warm flesh in his arms, and the burning blood of battle turned red hot, and—

One other woman only had made an impression upon him since his emergence from Death's quarters. She had no face, but he held an image of her in his imagination. Rask had spoken of his wife. When asked who he was, Rask spoke of the one he loved.

Zorsam hesitated. "Kiss me," Asundi whispered. But Zorsam lifted his head, as if awakened.

"He is fighting out there," he said. "I must join him."

"You've done enough," Asundi whispered. Her fingers played upon his muscled arm. "You judge and you take. Destroy and despoil. So, it shall be, Zorsam. So, you were destined."

He looked at her now. Her eyes were sly and alluring, and he could feel the soft curves through her ritual dress.

"You've rescued me," she said. "Come, enjoy your reward."

"I didn't do it for you."

She smiled. "I know that. You did it for yourself. You are strong enough to bend the world to your will. Bend me to it, Zorsam."

He could still hear the din of war outside. He could hear the swords and the screams. If Rask had not come the battle would have ended in slaughter. As it was, he did not know which side pressed forward and which fled. Asundi drew him close and the touch of her skin inflamed him so that he could hardly think, and yet the thoughts remained, stubborn, as if they were not his own.

"Your people are dying. Our people," he said, looking away from her. He could not look at her. He wanted to. If he did, he would never look away.

"The strong will survive, and you will lead them. Let the weak perish."

He remembered -- a man, dying painfully, outside the path from Death's keep. Zorsam had been newly born. He had slain the man, thinking it mercy. Perhaps it was, but he remembered, too, how Rask had tended his wounds, how Rask had followed after him on his little legs, always there, always eager, persistent, unstoppable, wounded and strong, insignificant and vital.

Zorsam stepped away, untangling himself from Asundi's grip. And he looked at her. Her face was stern and unforgiving. Her lithe form was made of iron and power. Behind her rose the statue of the wolf-god.

"You are the Destroyer," Asundi said. "Come ravish me."

"No. No!"

He stumbled as he backed away. In Asundi's aura, he had felt strong again, insatiably alive, but now his wounds and long series of fights were taking their toll.

"Then I will tear you to pieces and suck the marrow from your bones!"

Asundi launched herself at him. He threw his hands up to fend her off. He did not want to hurt her. A woman was not to be treated like a man, he sensed that much, and his mind was still overwhelmed with her strange femininity. Her fists struck with the force of a cudgel, and her nails ripped his skin. She moved with a wild fury, the likes of which Zorsam had never seen in a sane creature.

Desperate, he kicked her in the stomach, forcing some small distance between them. She lunged forward again, but he was ready. His arms closed around her and he squeezed, restraining her as she writhed. She craned her neck to tear at his flesh with her teeth, but he shifted to avoid them.

Strength failing, he squeezed, forcing air from her lungs, perhaps cracking ribs. He did not want to kill her; he did not want to free her. Though she was far smaller, her motions threatened to knock him off balance. He looked to Manrix, to the dark obsidian eyes. This place was the conduit. If Asundi left this place, would Manrix enter the world?

Kill her.

He did not know if it was his own thought or the subtle voice of Manrix. It did not matter. Whether a demon tempted him or his own conscience, he would not kill Asundi. Death had shown her to him. This was the reason. He was not just a sword. He could save as Rask had saved. Justice cost blood, and he would shed his instead of hers.

She would not relent. She was an unstoppable force. The battering reopened all his wounds. He fell to his knees but held on tight.

"I -- will—not -- release -- you."

His muscles burned. Soon, they would fail. With a fit of violent thrashing, she nearly freed an arm. Gritting his teeth, Zorsam tightened his embrace. It took all his will.

It was a useless battle. It accomplished nothing. He would release her, very soon.

"Asundi," he said, hardly able to speak because of his effort. "He heard you. I saw how you waited. The Great One. He sent me to you."

Asundi screeched and flailed and nearly broke free. Then, for a moment, she was still, a heavy weight in his tired arms. She spoke soft words he could barely hear.

"Destroy this place, Zorsam. Destroy it. Now."

Asundi collapsed in his embrace. His first instinct was to run. He could feel the pressure of Manrix's presence. It was dark and powerful and familiar. It was a force he could not long resist. But if he ran, he left Manrix's power unbroken to dwell in Asundi. Zorsam did not know how firm a grip the god had upon her, but it was not complete, not yet. Her brief lucidity showed that.

He set Asundi on the floor and felt the rough stone of the nearest pillar with his hands. He looked up its length, into darkness. The temple was not complete. If a support fell, would it still stand? He placed his palms on the stone, placed his feet for the best leverage, and pushed.

He might as well have pushed against a mountain. He pushed, his weary muscles straining, and moved not an inch. He stepped close, wrapped his arms around the pillar, set his good shoulder against it, and closed his eyes. He took a deep breath and then heaved.

He pulled away a moment later, sweating, dizzy. He opened his eyes to find the lights had gone out. He heard soft steps in the dark.

"Asundi!"

"You are in the maw. Soon the teeth will cut you to pieces. Run, barbarian, and tell your people that I come. Run, and tell them I will swallow the entire world. Run, you broken sword, and stumble upon your own blade."

Zorsam pressed his shoulder against the pillar again, forcing every muscle to work, forcing every ounce of will to the work. Still, beneath the effort, he heard the sharp sound of blade upon the tile floor. Asundi had found a sword.

"What is Zorsam the Great now?" she said. Her voice was deep and seductive and approaching. "With your arm you will slay armies? With your sword you will drain the enemy dry? If you had come to me, barbarian, if you had kissed me and made love to me, then we both would have dined and been satisfied."

Zorsam sucked in the warm air, chest heaving. He could see red behind his eyelids. "Great One," he whispered. "Use me." His limbs trembled uncontrollably, but he did not relent. "One time, use me."

He sensed the motion. A shock of clarity washed over him -- then the sword came out. He could not see his blood, but he could feel the hole. He screamed, blinded by the pain, insensible to the world. He screamed and roared and continued, with his last sane thoughts, to push.

A *crack* shook the world. He slipped and fell to the ground. The floor shuddered and the walls groaned, and he felt as if the Earth had begun to revolve more swiftly.

"What have you done?" Hands grabbed at him, searching for his face. "What have you done?"

Zorsam, blinking in the darkness, knew she was near. He reached out, hardly able to lift his arm, and grabbed her. He tugged at her clothes, and though she pulled away, his fingers held tight. He still had strength in his fingers, at least.

"Come," he said. "I'll take you to where Death lives."

She fell toward him, and he felt the weight of something heavy upon him, and his consciousness joined the darkness.

CHAPTER 16: Among Men

"Zorsam. Listen to me, Zorsam. You have saved us. You must live. You must come back to me. Do you understand? Can you understand what I'm saying?"

He heard the words as from far off, as if he lay buried in the grave, and the light above spoke to him. He could see nothing, but he felt water on his skin and a great weight and the presence of someone.

The voice spoke more words, but he could not understand them all. It was dark for a long time, and he heard scrambling and cries.

Then it was light -- he sensed it without opening his eyes -- and there was noise, an excited chattering, like birds singing and arguing in a tree. He could not distinguish the voices, and he wondered if they spoke a language unknown to him. Then he felt the soft flesh and heard the soft voice and he rose up from deep within, out of a well of isolation and pain. He opened his eyes, just a little, as much as he was able, and he saw her.

Asundi's proud, beautiful face smiled down at him and she spoke to him. "I've dug our way out. They're coming to help. Stay still."

"You are not Death."

She laughed, surprised. Death had never laughed. "No, I am alive, and so are you."

Zorsam struggled to sit, and though she told him not to, he managed to get his elbows under him so he could look around. He was in a small cavern of rubble. His legs were pinned, and he was caked in his own blood, but he could feel his extremities.

"Manrix is gone?"

Asundi's face stiffened. "Yes. I felt him being torn away from me. When the temple fell, it broke his hold. I can still remember what it felt like." She placed a hand on his arm. "I saw you in my dreams when Margruxks had me. You came for me."

Zorsam looked down. He could not look into those eyes. "The Great One sent me, but I didn't know what it meant. I thought strength was enough. I used his name, and he used me, but I don't know him."

"You do know him," Asundi said, smiling. "You only forgot him." She blinked, her eyes shining. "I hope you have not forgotten me?"

"I had. I am still a child in some ways."

She laughed. "And very much a man in others."

A shadow dimmed the light from outside their little cavern and a small man crawled in. "What? He's awake an' he ain't kissin' you yet? Zorsam, you got dem muscles, but yer head's full o' rocks."

Zorsam grinned at Rask's voice. He dared not speak, for his throat was suddenly tight.

Rask put his hands on his hips and surveyed the barbarian. "He got a tongue still, ain't he?"

"You live, Rask."

"Dat's right, I live. Dem Glaur soldiers kin't get ridda me dat easy. She tell you dey went scatterin' off when de temple fell? We already had dem on de defensive, den dis whole structure starts crumblin'. You shoulda seen der faces. White as death. So, we drives dem off."

Rask leaned forward, hands on his knees. "Dat's two nations freed in one day. Fancy dat, Zorsam? Even de basement held steady 'til we gots de women an' younguns out. Dat Great One came through, didn't he? An' you's still here, too. Guess nufin's ever gonna kill you. How 'bout we finds a way ta get dat leg unpinned?"

Rask summoned a few other Garr men, and they crowded into the tight space. Soon, they had Zorsam's leg free. He was not sure he could put weight on it, and the space was too small for him to stand. Rask hurried out first, followed by the other Garr men. Asundi followed behind Zorsam as he worked his way through the tight tunnel, pulling himself forward with his arms. The rock pressed against his shoulder and back, squeezing him. Ahead, he could see light.

The tunnel compressed him until he could hardly breathe. Rask bent down and reached in to grab his arm. With his help, Zorsam emerged.

Standing unsteadily in the morning light, supported by Rask and Asundi, he saw Shamgar and Manoah and a large crowd of men and women waiting on the shattered steps just below him.

Rask placed something on his head. "Found it on de battlefield. Figured you'd show up eventually."

Zorsam reached up and felt the matted, bloodied fur of the lion's mane.

"All hail, Chieftain Zorsam!" Shamgar shouted. The others took up the chant.

Zorsam looked down at Asundi.

"We have waited a long time for you, Zorsam," she said.

"I did not even know I was waiting for you."

The crowd cheered as Asundi stood upon her toes and placed a gentle kiss upon his lips. "Welcome back, Zorsam."

END

ABOUT THE AUTHORS

Nick Hayden is a writer, a podcaster, a teacher, and a father. He has written novels, short stories, and more than 100 flash fictions, most of which are available at www.worksofnick.com. He is also the co-host of Derailed Trains of Thought, a podcast about storytelling for the creator and consumer. He teaches middle school English, where he tortures his students with his red pen. He is married to the lovely Natasha and spends his free time with his three children.

Nathan Joseph Sitton Marchand is a writer, grad student, podcaster, and teacher hailing from northeastern Indiana. He is the author/co-author of multiple short stories, articles, and books (including the novella *Destroyer*, which was created as part of the same project that birthed Zorsam). One of his many current projects is The Monster Island Film Vault, a film appreciation podcast focused on giant monster movies (i.e., dai kaiju eiga). In his spare time, his other creative endeavors include gaming, photography, acting, ballroom dancing, and occasionally saving the world. His website is www.NathanJSMarchand.com.

Aaron Michael Brosman is a game designer from Northeastern Indiana. He is also a comics lover, animation fanboy, and general purpose nerd. Normally found in his natural habitat – online playing video games – Aaron surrounds himself with board games and RPG books. His fondest wish is that you find your joy in life! Well, what are you waiting for?

96